DEVOTED DOGS

Sue Welford

Illustrated by
Trevor Newton

Hodder
Children's
Books

A division of Hodder Headline plc

Text copyright © 1999 Sue Welford
Illustrations copyright © 1999 Trevor Newton

First published in Great Britain in 1999
by Hodder Children's Books

A Catalogue record for this book is available from the British Library

ISBN 0 340 74421 9

Typeset by Avon Dataset Ltd, Bidford-on-Avon, Warks

Printed and bound in Great Britain by
The Guernsey Press Co. Ltd, Guernsey, Channel Isles

Hodder Children's Books
a division of Hodder Headline plc
338 Euston Road
London NW1 3BH

This book is dedicated to
Blue, Rattie, Jess, Ryka, Tazz,
Muffet, Midge, Chloe and Milo,
devoted dogs past and present

Acknowledgements

Thanks to:

Lesley Pollinger
Canine Search and Rescue
Natural History Museum, Berne
Allan Frewin
Ashford Library

for their help in researching this book.

Contents

RATS
the Soldier Dog

No-one knew where he came from, who his parents were, or if he belonged to anyone. They didn't even know if he had a name. But the little Corgi/Jack Russell type stray dog that roamed the streets of Crossmaglen in Northern Ireland was destined to become a symbol of survival for the British soldiers serving there.

It was a dark and dismal wintertime when the 42 Commando Royal Marines occupied a service base in Crossmaglen, County Armagh, during the height of the Troubles. As usual in that part of Ulster, there were lots of stray dogs haunting the perimeter of the base. Whether they were hoping to be fed or were trying to fulfil some doggie need for human company, no-one really knew.

The base was pretty basic. It was a long narrow building that adjoined the old police station with offices, sleeping quarters and a cookhouse. The soldiers were dry and warm but they were a long way from their homes and families and the building often seemed stark and unwelcoming.

The little dog, Rats, as he later became known, was living on a piece of waste ground near the perimeter fence. This derelict ground was his territory and he guarded it fiercely from the other stray dogs who wandered around, some twice his size. Although he lived in the open, he seemed healthy enough. His rough, thick coat kept him warm on cold winter days, when sleet and snow blew through the village and the ground was as hard as iron. He could run like the wind on his short legs. His bright eyes were sharp and quick to spot danger. Maybe it was his cocky ears, his stubby, perky tail, his jaunty way of walking that first attracted the men to him. Whatever it was, Rats felt the same as they did. He loved soldiers and they, in turn, were to fall in love with him.

The first real contact with the little dog came when a contingent from the base was out on patrol one cold, blustery day. Suddenly, from nowhere, a scruffy little dog trotted cheekily towards them and began attacking the men's bootlaces. He thought it was a great game. Growling and tugging, he managed to undo several pairs before he felt the side of a soldier's boot and scampered away to watch from a distance.

Even though they'd sent him off, the men hadn't

failed to notice what a cute fellow the little dog was. For someone who was no more than ten centimetres or so off the ground, attacking soldiers' bootlaces seemed a brave act indeed. In fact, for men under constant threat from terrorist snipers and bombs, attention from such a friendly little creature was welcome.

And so Rats wormed his way into the soldiers' affections. The next time he appeared, the half-hearted kicks gave way to pats on the head. Every time he saw them coming, Rats would run and bark and play. With no reward but a friendly word or pat, he had decided the soldiers belonged to him. If any other dogs tried to make friends too he saw them off. Hackles up, growling and barking more fiercely than any Alsatian; even the biggest dog fled in terror.

It wasn't long before Rats was going everywhere with the soldiers. In his doggie mind they were his friends, his companions, the family he'd never had. But he wasn't content with that – he wanted to make himself useful, too.

The first sign that Rats wanted to be a real soldier came when, out on patrol, he began to growl at any sign, scent or sight of approaching strangers. Where round every corner there could be a gun-toting terrorist and every tree or bush could be hiding an unseen, deadly enemy, Rats became a star scout. Soon he was a vital member of the Commando force and when the soldiers discovered he didn't belong to anybody, to his great joy they allowed him into the base. To Rats, this was doggie heaven. He abandoned his precious piece of waste ground without a backward glance. A blanket, warmth, food, what more could a fellow want? Someone gave him a bath and groomed him free of fleas. An army doctor checked him over and declared him fit for duty. Although he had no particular master, everyone was his friend.

No-one quite knew when or by whom Rats had been given his name. Some said the word was short for 'rations' because one of the dog's favourite places was the cookhouse . . . another that he was called Rats because when they first saw him he reminded them of a scruffy, flea-bitten rat. But whoever had given it to him, the name suited him down to the ground.

The friendship of the little dog became very important to the soldiers. He reminded them of their own dogs and in a strange way, the comforts of home.

Meanwhile he was still up to his old tricks. The bootlace attack was brilliant fun. Fetching stones and putting them by feet so they could be kicked and brought back again was another great game. Rushing around and barking at the envious strays lurking around the perimeter fence, only came second to chasing any vehicle that dared to drive past.

Then, one day, Rats spotted something that was to become the best game of all.

Later, he was to develop a passion for helicopters but for the moment, the Saracen armoured cars were his target. Every time he spotted one on the move he would run and bark and try to bite at the wheels. Scared they would run the little dog down, the drivers would stop. This was exactly what he wanted. One flying leap and he was in the back. Often he just wanted to curl up and go to sleep, other times he would sit up with the driver and enjoy being the highest and most important dog in town.

But Rats was soon to learn a lesson. Being a soldier wasn't all being top dog and riding high in armoured cars. It was more than going out on patrol or lying in the mess at night with a full stomach and friends for company. More than simply protecting and giving loyalty and affection to your fellow servicemen.

It meant danger, real danger and a risk to your life.

It was on a freezing cold day that Rats went out on patrol as usual. There were some new faces in camp. A detachment from the 2nd Company, 1st Battalion Grenadier Guards had arrived. Although Rats didn't know it, they were to take over from his beloved Royal Marines. Two of these new soldiers went with the two Marines out on patrol. For the newcomers, it was hard to believe that the quiet, country village of Crossmaglen could be under the menace of terrorist attack. But it was, and they were soon to learn just how deadly the dangers were.

They left the base with Rats as usual trotting on

ahead. He had appointed himself official look-out for the army patrols and always went first to sniff for danger. As the five soldiers got near a derelict house it was noticed that there was fresh earth dug around a telegraph pole. This looked menacing and dangerous. Often mines were concealed a few centimetres below the surface of the soil. The sergeant ordered them to cross to safety on the other side of the road. This meant walking next to the derelict building. Usually these were avoided as they were easy places to plant explosives. This time, though, the house had been checked and the soldiers thought they were safe. But they weren't. As they passed by, a massive blast ripped the air. Two metal gas containers full of explosives had been detonated by radio control just as the soldiers went by.

After the explosion, everything was chaotic. The air was thick with smoke and debris. The soldiers had been deafened by the blast and couldn't hear the screams of wounded men, the wild yelping of an injured dog. It was as if the end of the world had come.

One soldier died in that attack, another two were wounded. In the savage confusion of the moment, Rats was forgotten. The time hadn't yet come when his survival was as important to the men as that of their own.

Later, when it was noticed he was gone, the soldiers were horrified and upset. Their little pal had been blown up by a terrorist bomb. They would never see him again.

It was while the Company Commander was examining the area that he came across a trail of blood. He was surprised when it led back to the base. As far as he knew, the wounded men had been flown to hospital. Then he remembered the little dog he had often spotted going out on patrol. He asked around. To his great relief he learned Rats had been found by one of the soldiers and was in the medical room getting treatment. He had been badly wounded and had crawled away to try to recover on his own. He had a hole in his side and both his ears were torn and tattered.

At the hands of the army medics, Rats got all the loving care that any human would have done in the same circumstances. For days he wouldn't eat and it seemed to the men that he might die. They had found him only to lose him again. The sergeant who had discovered him had to force feed him at times. For Rats, for the small community of soldiers, things were looking grim.

But thanks to the efforts of that sergeant, Rats got better. From that time he became *his* dog. He patrolled with him, staying at heel, dropping down on his belly and waiting until he was ordered to move again. The sergeant was enchanted by the little dog's intelligence. Suddenly life amongst the dangers of Northern Ireland wasn't so bad after all. And as for Rats? He might have lost bits of his ears, he might have scars, but he had lost none of his courage. And at last he had one master he could call his very own.

It was about this time that Rats developed his love of helicopters. No-one quite knew why. Maybe it was because he was so short. His view of life was from shin height, a forest of boots and trouser legs. Up in the air he could be a king. One day he followed his sergeant on to a helicopter and refused to budge. He'd got a master now and he was going to hang on to him. Later, he could be seen jumping on to any helicopter that was taking off. Rats didn't care where it was going. One flying leap and he was there. Often he had to stay the night at another base and would be returned the next day. No-one seemed to mind. In fact a visit from the soldier dog was the highlight of their day.

But things were to change and it was a sad day for Rats when the change of duty came round. His battalion's stint in Ulster was over and Rats was to lose the sergeant who had saved his life when he had been so badly wounded. The brave little dog's beloved master and the soldiers he had come to love and respect were to return home to the safe shores of England. He wasn't allowed to go with them so instead he was handed over to the incoming battalion in the hope they would love and care for him as much as the old one had done. And that he, in turn, would be faithful to them.

For a while Rats was miserable. He couldn't

understand why his sergeant and his other friends had left. He didn't know they had parents and wives and families to go back to. They probably even had dogs of their own. He felt deserted. What had he done wrong to make them go away?

But gradually his cheerfulness returned. The new men were just as kind. There were different soldiers, new patrols to go out with. Rats didn't know it but there were to be three changes in the battalions that served in Crossmaglen while he was a serving soldier. He accepted, protected and loved each one.

Word of the little dog soldier had spread in Northern Ireland and British Intelligence sources learned that the Irish Republican Army wanted to kill him. They knew that losing the little dog would upset the soldiers' morale. As a result, more care was taken always to know where Rats was. It was important to keep him safe. In spite of this, though, the little dog was wounded again. His tail was burned away when a firebomb exploded while he was out on patrol with the Queen's Own Highlanders. Later X-rays showed he had bits of shrapnel in his body. Still, Rats soldiered on, protecting and comforting the men he adored. They had lost count of how many times he had been shot at. In fact a shotgun pellet remained lodged in his chest for ever.

By now, his fame had spread beyond Northern Ireland. There were stories about him in the newspapers and he even got letters written to him by people from England. One summer a TV crew arrived to film the soldiers. They found Rats and as a result he became a TV star. Everyone loved him, his warmth and his cheeky personality. The army became more aware than ever what a loyal and faithful dog he was and how the men relied on him to cheer them up when they were feeling lonely and afraid.

In honour of this it was decided that Rats should get an army number of his very own. A medal was made, a dog-disc with the Queen's head on one side and his number on the other. '*Rats. Delta 777*'. Delta was for the Delta Company that was serving in Ulster at the time and the three sevens were considered lucky.

Rats received his medal at a special ceremony when it was pinned to his collar while a piper played Scotland the Brave. Even the hardest of the men wiped away a tear. Rats was their buddy, their companion, a brave soldier. They were proud of him.

It soon became obvious, however, that Rats' health wasn't good. He had been injured several times, run over twice in the course of his duties. He had also suffered wounds from fighting off much bigger dogs who had been encouraged by their masters to attack the troops. If that wasn't enough he'd got stomach problems from a diet that wasn't all a dog's diet should be. He would wander through the base, getting tit-bits wherever he went. Steak, sausages, cakes from the cook. Chocolate and chips from the men. Rats was sick a lot and although he was still full of enthusiasm and energy it was sometimes obvious he wasn't the dog he used to be.

Then, just before Christmas some exciting news came from England. Rats had been awarded a Gold Medal from a charity called PRO Dogs. He was to be their 'Dog of the Year'.

So, at the height of his army career, Rats travelled to London to receive his medal. It was the longest flight he'd ever been on.

Before the ceremony he appeared on TV with his friend Corporal Lewis who had travelled with him to London. Then he went to the awards dinner where he was to be given his medal. There were lots of other dogs there. Some had won prizes at dog shows, some were loyal family pets, others had done brave deeds. They were all 'posh dogs', groomed and sleek. They seemed to look down their noses at Rats as if to say *what are you doing here?*'. But Rats didn't care. He might be a scruffy little mongrel with short legs and tatty ears but inside that little chest beat the biggest, bravest heart in the world.

When the medal on a tartan ribbon was put round his neck Rats barked his thanks.

After that he was more famous than ever. People wrote him more letters and sent him gifts of toys and bones. There were Christmas cards by the hundred. But fame didn't go to his head. He carried on doing his duty as if he wasn't a star at all. All he really wanted was to be a faithful friend and companion to his fellow soldiers.

In spite of all this, it was becoming more and more obvious that all was not well with the little soldier dog. Before he went to London for his medal he had been taken to the Army Dog Veterinary Officer for a check up. The vet had reported he was very run down. He was suffering from blood poisoning from a rat bite and his paws were in bad condition. It has to be remembered that Rats wasn't a pampered pet living in a cosy home. He was a working soldier, out in all weathers, up to his belly in dirt and continually under stress from the dangers and horrors of war.

By now, he was about eight. Approximately fifty-six years in human terms. His medical examination had shown a heart condition and he often seemed exhausted from jumping in and out of helicopters or armoured cars. He still chased vehicles but wasn't as quick as he used to be at getting out of the way. Everyone was afraid, if he didn't rest, he would die. Being a good soldier was taking its toll.

And so it was decided that Rats, the soldier dog, should be retired with honour. A home in England was found for him. A place where he could be safe and get back his health.

But Rats would not disappear from the army scene quietly. He had served in one of the most uncertain and threatening parts of the world longer than any other soldier. The British army wanted to honour him. In the future, other dogs might attach themselves to soldiers. Other dogs would serve. But it was doubted that any would be as loyal, as merry, as friendly and as bright as Rats. Or that any would be loved so much.

It was a grand day when the Prince of Wales' Company, 1st Battalion Welsh Guards, in full dress uniform assembled for Rats' retirement ceremony. Wives, children and friends were watching as he was brought out with his escort. He walked the long line of soldiers without once pouncing on their bootlaces. He knew that on this important day of his life he must behave himself. A final helicopter ride had been arranged and when it landed, Rats dashed across the parade ground and launched himself joyfully into it almost as if he could fly.

Months later, when Rats had settled down in his new home, he may have thought of that last, thrilling helicopter ride that brought him to safety and back to good health. Maybe, lying in the warm sunshine surrounded by the love of his new family he might have wished he was back in his old soldiering days. Maybe he looked at his medal, in pride of place on the family's mantelpiece, and thought of his time in Crossmaglen. And even if, in time, he forgot, it's certain that the soldiers he served with never forgot him. One of them once said of him: 'He was an oasis of friendship in a desert of sadness'. A great thing to say about Rats – the brave soldier dog.

GREYFRIARS BOBBY
the Dog who never gave up

There are lots of myths and legends about the little Skye terrier who came to be known as Greyfriars Bobby but searches among true historical records have now told the real story of the amazing dog.

It was during the reign of Queen Victoria, over a hundred years ago that a Mr John Gray, sometimes known as 'Auld Jock', came from the country to the city of Edinburgh, Scotland, to find work. There had been terrible storms that year, the fields were flooded and the crops ruined. Many men and women who worked on the land were unable to get jobs. Jock was one of these people and he brought his wife and son to the city hoping to find work as a gardener. But all the gardening jobs had been taken and so it was then that he decided to become a policeman.

There weren't any exams to pass in those days.

All Jock had to do was visit the inspector of police for an interview. The inspector decided Jock would make a good policeman and he started straight away. Jock was overjoyed. His wife and son were starving and they lived in the poorest part of the city. Now, things were looking up.

In those days, most policemen had dogs to go with them on their beat. These dogs weren't the highly trained, pedigree dogs they are today. In fact any well-behaved dog who would warn you of approaching strangers would do. A dog was assigned to Jock. Part of Jock's beat was a dark and sinister graveyard called Greyfriars. It was the haunt of thieves and ruffians and Jock felt much safer with some company.

No-one quite knows when or how Jock lost his first dog but when he disappeared he was quickly replaced by the friendly Skye Terrier called Bobby. Bobby was a very small dog with long hair, big feet for his size, perky ears and bright eyes peering out from under long shaggy eyebrows. John was charmed the minute he first saw him.

Terriers make ideal watch dogs. They have a keen sense of smell and can scent through several layers of soil. Their name comes from the Latin word *terra* meaning 'earth'.

Bobby proved to be a great pal. He stayed close to his master's side and loved going out on patrol with him. The tall policeman and his little dog soon became a familiar sight in the area.

There were three busy markets in Edinburgh in those days and often when John had finished night duty at the cattle market he would return to a place called Hall's Court and stop at a coffee house near Greyfriars Palace. The policeman's duty at the market was to keep an eye on the livestock left there overnight and prevent any being stolen. The owner of the coffee shop was always pleased to see Jock and Bobby when they came off duty and they had their own special seat.

There would always be a hot meal for Jock and a bun or a meaty bone for Bobby and a pat and a friendly word from soldiers from the local garrison.

Although part of Jock's beat was in a poor and dangerous part of the city, not many minutes' walk from there was a park called Holyrood Park where people could enjoy fresh air and sunshine. By the time summer came, Bobby had grown used to his duties and stuck close to his master on their walks around the city. He loved going to the park with Jock, to enjoy the green turf and the banks of summer flowers that grew there. Bobby loved to run and chase the rabbits and make the most of the freedom of the park after the dim darkness of the narrow alleys of the city.

Bobby was proving to be highly intelligent. He knew what 'walkies' meant and 'bone' and would sit and stay when the command 'on trust' was given. He would never move until Jock gave him permission. He would often lie patiently at his master's feet beside the other policemen and their dogs watching the soldiers drilling, up and down, up and down to the commands of their Superintendent. Jock was always pleased with the way Bobby behaved and reckoned he'd got one of the best watch dogs in the force.

When winter came and the days were cold and wet, Bobby and his master would often arrive home soaked through to the skin. Jock's wife always had a good fire going and they would sit there shivering while they dried out. However, one day Jock became ill with a nasty cough that wouldn't go away and although Bobby thought the sound was strange at first he soon got used to it. Jock became too ill and weak to go out on his beat and his bed was brought downstairs so that he could be by the fire. Bobby would lay on his blanket staring at his master and wondering why he didn't get up so they could both go out on duty.

As the winter days passed, Jock didn't get any better. He lay under his covers, shivering and sweating. By Christmas, his cough was much worse and the doctor told his wife he had a bad lung infection that sadly could not be cured.

As Jock was no longer fit for duty, Bobby was confused. Why was his master lying in bed all day instead of going out on his beats round the busy markets? He lay unhappily on his blanket by the fire still waiting and hoping that his master would soon be able to go back to work.

But Auld Jock did not recover from his illness and even though he did manage to take Bobby for one or two walks, two months after Christmas Bobby's beloved master died.

When people came to put Jock into a funny wooden box Bobby whimpered with fear. Why were they taking his master away when there was work to be done?

On the day of Jock's funeral Bobby followed the procession through the market, up Candlemakers Row and through the burial gate at Greyfriars. Bobby watched sadly as the coffin was lowered into the ground and covered with earth. He couldn't understand why they had put his master in such a dark place where he couldn't see him. He wondered how long it would be before his master was up and about again and they could go back to work.

As everyone turned to go, Bobby lay down beside the grave, his nose on his paws, waiting. Then he found himself being lifted up and very firmly taken home. The cemetery was no place for a little dog all on his own.

Jock's family and friends gathered at the house after the funeral. Bobby was still confused. Why were all these people here and where was his master? For the first time in his life the little dog raised his nose to the sky and howled. After that he waited a while then began scratching at the door to go out. At last someone opened it for him and he was away, running down the stairs and out into the yard, along the dirty streets towards Greyfriars as fast as his little legs would go. He *had* to find his master.

But when Bobby got to the churchyard he couldn't get in. The gates had been locked for the night. He scrabbled about, trying to get underneath, digging frantically with his paws. Then he stopped, cocked his head and listened. The church bells were ringing ten o'clock. It was time for the police patrol.

As soon as the patrol arrived and unlocked the gate, Bobby hurtled through. He knew exactly where his master lay. He could scent him from under the earth. When he found the grave he lay down quietly. Even when the rain started and the wind began to

moan around the gravestones Bobby stayed where he was. Luckily, Auld Jock had been buried close to two huge table-stones and it was there that Bobby eventually took shelter when the rain and wind got too much to bear. There, he curled up and went to sleep. He was staying 'on trust' just as his master had commanded him to do so many times.

Some time after sunrise, a man called James Brown came to unlock the gate. When he spotted Bobby he yelled at him and shook his fist. Dogs definitely weren't allowed in the churchyard. But when he tried to pick Bobby up and take him out of the churchyard the little dog growled and tried to bite his hands. Although Bobby was only small he had very sharp teeth. He was guarding his master and no-one was going to interfere. Bobby became so angry he ran at the man, snapping at his shoes and trouser legs. James was just wondering what to do when the man in charge of the churchyard came and recognised Bobby. He told James about the little dog and James felt sorry then for he knew that Bobby was staying faithfully beside his master. He decided to leave him there for the time being. He thought Bobby would soon give up and realise his master was never coming back.

But James was wrong. The weeks went by and Bobby stayed firmly beside the grave. At last, James gave up trying to move him. Bobby was staying faithful to Auld Jock – he was his master and the little dog *had* to stay by his side. So instead of trying to remove him, James began feeding Bobby. He even put a blanket under the old stone table for the little terrier to lie on.

Winter turned to spring and Bobby was still there. When the night policemen patrolled the area they remembered Bobby had been their comrade's dog and they would leave him tit-bits from their lunch boxes. But even though he was being fed, the local people knew that Bobby would find it hard to survive on his own once spring and summer turned to winter again.

When Jock's wife and son visited the grave they tried to make Bobby come home but if they did carry him back to the house he would whine and scratch at the door until they let him out. The last they would see of him would be his shaggy tail waving in the air as he ran off as fast as he could towards the Greyfriars churchyard where his beloved master lay.

Then another man named James, James Anderson, took pity on Bobby and one stormy night he went down to Greyfriars and at last managed to persuade Bobby to come home with him. Bobby was cold and wet where the storm had blown the rain under his shelter and the man had a kind voice that reminded him of his master. Maybe it would be a good idea to be indoors by a cosy fire on such a terrible night.

Mr Anderson lived near the graveyard and Bobby was soon lying on a blanket by the man's warm hearth. Bobby still wondered what had happened to his master and why he had never come out of his strange bed to talk to him. But he didn't worry too much. Even though he was beside another man's fire, he was still close to the place where his master lay and that was all that really mattered.

Bobby stayed at Mr Anderson's house all winter. The people next door often took him in too and he would enjoy a meal in their house and a warm bed on cold winter nights. Bobby knew which side his bread was buttered. He was being looked after but he was never very far from Jock. He often called in at an eating house where he used to go with his master and there he would be given a meal and a drink. But as soon as the weather got better he would always return to sit by the grave and wait.

By now, Bobby was becoming quite well known. People would stare and point as he trotted past on his way to one of his friends' houses or the restaurant. He became known as Greyfriars Bobby and everyone admired him for his loyalty and courage. As autumn came Bobby loved to chase the leaves in the churchyard and in winter he would play in the snow. Greyfriars now belonged to him and he would chase away any visiting dogs or cats.

When Bobby had been guarding his master's grave for four years, a great change came over his life. Because, in those days, not everyone had watches or clocks, the custom used to be to fire a cannon at one o'clock every day so people would know exactly what time it was. One o'clock was just about the time that Bobby would trot away from Greyfriars to go to Currie's Eating House, one of the places where he would get lunch. He had a friend there, Sergeant Scott who was stationed at Edinburgh Castle. When the sergeant had heard about Bobby he made a special effort to become his friend. Every week he would buy him a steak dinner and he often took him for walks, showing him off to the other soldiers. The sergeant's regiment was to be put in charge of firing the time-gun and Bobby was allowed to stand and watch. Bobby soon realised that his soldier friend went for his lunch after the gun had been discharged and it became a signal for him to go for his dinner too.

Soon, this event became a daily routine and often a small crowd of people would come to see Bobby trot off for his dinner a few seconds after one o'clock. They would point and laugh and it seemed Bobby knew this. He would trot along with his little head held high. Bobby was becoming a star. Many people would go to the graveyard too, to see him guarding his master's grave. This appealed to the Victorian people. They liked to hear stories of loyalty and kindness and they hoped that when they died, someone would be as faithful to their memory as Greyfriars Bobby was to the memory of his dead master.

By now, Bobby was about six years old and although he didn't realise it, his life suddenly became under threat. At that time, it was a strict law that every dog had to be licensed. And although Bobby had lots of friends, no-one actually owned him. Stray, unlicensed dogs were rounded up and taken away to be destroyed. Was this going to happen to Bobby after all his years of faithful vigil?

The Lord Provost of Edinburgh, a very important man, heard about Bobby. He was very fond of dogs and was charmed by the story of the little terrier. He asked that Bobby be brought to see him. He loved and admired the little dog and immediately paid for his licence. The kind man also had a special collar made for him. It had a brass plate with the words '*Greyfriars Bobby from the Lord Provost, 1867, licensed*' inscribed on it. To everyone's relief, Bobby was safe.

Meanwhile, Bobby's fame was spreading. Artists came to sketch and paint him, there were stories about him in many newspapers, not only in Scotland but all over the country. People came from everywhere to see him sitting by Auld Jock's grave. All this fame didn't go to Bobby's head. He simply carried on as normal. Sitting by the grave on fair days, trotting to the eating house on the dot of one o'clock each day and visiting various friends and restaurants where he knew he would be fed.

In November 1871 Bobby had his sixteenth birthday. He had now been guarding his master's burial place for thirteen years. Bobby was growing weak and could no longer lie out in all weathers.

One cold night, two of his friends, Anne Mackay and Agnes Cunningham who helped out at the coffee shop, took Bobby indoors to be by their fire. That night he fell asleep and didn't wake up. His long vigil at his master's side was over.

Bobby was buried under a tree in front of the old Greyfriars Church and even today he is still remembered with love and affection by the people of Edinburgh. There are several things connected with him that can still be seen today. A fountain with a statue of Bobby sits at the top of Candlemakers Row. The plaque on the fountain reads '*A tribute to the affectionate fidelity of Greyfriars Bobby . . .*' A group of Americans who had visited Greyfriars collected money to erect a memorial stone over Auld Jock's grave that commemorates Bobby too and Bobby's collar and his metal dinner dish can be seen at the Huntly House Museum in Edinburgh.

No-one knows the exact spot in front of the church where the terrier was buried on that cold winter's day in 1872 but he is close to the grave of Auld Jock. What we do know is that Greyfriars Bobby still keeps guard over his beloved master in death just as he did for the seventeen brave and faithful years of his life.

MOOBLI
the Wilderness Dog

When naturalist and photographer Mike Tomkies first saw Moobli, the Alsatian puppy was fat and weird looking with feet that were too big, knock-knees and floppy ears. When he moved, his paws went flip-flop on the ground. As Mike picked him up, Moobli pushed his big, black, wet nose into his ear and gave him a slobbery kiss. *Well*, thought Mike, who wanted a rough, tough dog to share his life in the wilds of remote Scotland, *he's friendly anyway.*

Mike had lived and travelled to many wild places in the world but it was only when he came to Scotland that he decided he needed a comrade to share his lonely life. But even as he agreed to take the Alsatian puppy, he was having second thoughts. Would Moobli prove to be the hardy companion he needed? Somehow he doubted it.

Little did Mike know, though, that Moobli would

become more than just a companion. He would become his best pal, his helper and his faithful friend and during their time together in the small cottage near a wild loch in Scotland, miles from anywhere, the Alsatian would twice save his life.

The dog breeder had assured Mike that Moobli would grow into a handsome, intelligent and faithful beast. Mike was still dubious. The puppy seemed to have no brain. It chased birds, ran away when it saw other dogs and was scared of boats. If it was to live in a remote place and face the dangers of the wilderness life then it would have to change. Mike needed more than just a companion, he wanted a dog to track wildlife for his photography, to help him and protect him if needed. But when, a few weeks later, Moobli ran away, tail between his legs, from a ram that had come to the house to be fed, he almost gave up. This dog was a coward, he would never shape up. He phoned the breeder and asked if she would take him back. The breeder told Mike to have patience. All the puppy needed was lots of love and affection . . . and time.

Meanwhile Moobli was finding it hard to settle down. As far as he was concerned, things had got off to a very bad start. He had hated the long drive from one end of the country to the other. He didn't know how horrible cars could be. The long journey was the first one he had ever been on. He had been sick and his new master wasn't very pleased at having to clear up the mess. He was petrified of monster trucks screaming past them on the motorway. When they stopped at service stations, the noise, the hustle and bustle of people was too much for him. He dived between Mike's legs and wanted to stay there for ever.

Mike was relieved when the long journey to Scotland was over too. He hadn't realised the dog would be ill and scared. He was still having doubts about him. He travelled a lot and a dog that was sick and frightened of cars wouldn't be much use to him at all.

After that first journey, Moobli soon discovered there were new horrors to be faced. A long, choppy boat trip to the small cottage that was to be his home. The stretch of stormy water seemed endless. Then there were great, dark mountains looming overhead. Moobli's first glimpse of his new home from the bouncing, rocking bow of the small boat was too much for him. He dived into the cabin and hid, trembling. He must have wished a thousand times he was back with his brothers and sisters in the cosy kennel where he had been born.

Gradually, though, things began to change. As Moobli settled down in his new home, he found he was starting to enjoy car rides and boat trips in the waters of the loch. He got over his sickness and his fear. He loved looking out of the car window and he learned to swim and to run and play. He loved the long walks with Mike along the shore, through woods and marshlands, through forests of bracken, over rocks and across icy, turbulent rivers. There were no sedate outings in the park for this pooch, no trots along the pavement. Moobli was destined to be a wilderness dog whether he liked it or not.

Moobli soon discovered there were lots of things to play with in his new home. Sticks and conkers, stones and the toys his master made for him. There were birds, squirrels and rabbits to chase. At night, curled up by the fire, Moobli decided that life in the wilderness was going to be great after all.

As the bond between the naturalist and the Alsatian grew stronger, Moobli began to prove what a good choice he had been. He learned to be quiet when Mike was stalking deer. He learned to stay, when to run and when to be still. He tracked all kinds of wildlife for Mike to photograph. Badgers, foxes, birds, even otters along the shores. He would sniff their scent long before Mike could spot any sign of them, warning his master of their presence. No rough ground was too much of a challenge for Moobli. He would trek steadily and fearlessly through the thickest forest, climb mountains, swim the deep waters of the loch. Whatever Mike asked of him, he never let him down.

By now, Moobli was huge and very strong. He had a broad, golden chest and dark muzzle and ears. The huge paws he'd had as a puppy carried him along at enormous speed, on land and in the water. His powerful jaws could have torn a man's arm off. In spite of that he was gentle as a lamb with the wild creatures Mike rescued. He once sniffed out an injured fawn and lay beside it until Mike arrived on the scene. He made friends with a young owl that Mike had found and taken home to look after until it was old enough to fend for itself. The dog would lie quietly and watch birds eat the food Mike had put out for them and never try to chase them. He was a brilliant tracker and could easily sniff out herds of red deer, keeping back on command by Mike's side so they weren't frightened off. He was thrilled by the sight of flying birds and would sit and watch them wheeling and diving in the sky.

Moobli was turning out to be just the kind of dog Mike had dreamed of. He had grown to love him so much that when he had to leave him with a friend and take a trip abroad he was scared the dog would forget him. If he didn't recognise Mike on his return he thought it would break his heart.

But he need not have worried. When he came home Moobli was waiting. He jumped into Mike's Land Rover without a backward glance or a lick of thanks for the man who had looked after him. Then the Alsatian leapt on to the boat and stood in the bow with a grin on his face . . . they were going home.

But a huge test was to come. Mike had studied wild cats in Canada and when he got back from a trip someone offered him two wild kittens. Although wild cats used to roam the whole of Britain, they're now only found in the north of

Scotland. They are fierce, spiteful and untameable. How would the great Alsatian dog take to two wild companions sharing his small wilderness cottage? Mike decided only time would tell.

When they were first introduced, the huge dog stared at the kittens in surprise and wonder. What were these furry, spitting things his master had brought into the house? When he sniffed them and they spat and lashed out with their claws, his pride was hurt. He slunk to his blanket in a sulk.

Mike wanted the new arrivals to stay as wild as possible so he built them a home outside. Moobli would go and watch them, fascinated as they romped together. Mike made sure he still cuddled Moobli. If the dog became jealous of the kittens he could kill them with one chop of his mighty jaws if he wanted to. Soon, though, Moobli had accepted them as part of the family. It was this grace and nobility that Mike loved so much. He knew he had a dog in a million.

Moobli was to make lots more friends out of wild creatures during his time in the wilderness. His marvellous tracking skills got better and better. He scented other wild cats that visited, he helped Mike discover the homes and territories of foxes and badgers so Mike could keep a record of their movements. Mike became convinced Moobli could read his mind. He seemed to know what he wanted before he was asked. Mike knew that, without this incredible dog, he would never have been able to make his unique photographic record of the wildlife of the Scottish Highlands. He knew also that the loneliness of their remote home would have been unbearable without him. Moobli was his companion, his helper, his best friend.

All the time they were together, Moobli never stopped amazing his master. He climbed mountain crags to find eagles' nests, he fought off a huge stag that attacked them one day when they were walking in the forest. Mike loved him for his courage, his strength and most of all, his intelligence. How could he ever have thought that Moobli didn't have a brain!

And it was a combination of Moobli's intelligence and strength that saved Mike's life one fateful autumn day. Mike, Moobli and one of the wild cats, Liane, were returning from a trip to London. Moobli and Liane were now the best of friends and the cat had been company for the dog when Mike had to leave them for business meetings.

As they were about to head home along the loch a storm blew up. Mike loaded the boat with provisions, started the engine and they set off. The water was rough and it wasn't long before they were getting swamped. Then the engine cut out and they were being tossed around helplessly. To Mike's horror he suddenly realised they were sinking. There seemed to be only one thing to do. Abandon ship! Mike leaped out, clutching the cat's cage in one hand, his briefcase with precious notes and papers in the other. Moobli was already in the water, paddling around and snorting like a channel swimming bear. Mike was struggling to stay afloat in five metres of icy water when he called out desperately to his dog. 'Come here, Moobli! Come here!'

Moobli sped strongly towards them. Mike grabbed his tail with the hand that clutched the briefcase and the dog hauled them all ashore, swimming bravely through the surging waves that sometimes broke right over his head. Mike kicked out madly, the cat's box held high to stop it going under the water. On dry land at last, Mike lay gasping for air, the panting courageous dog beside him. Moobli had saved their lives.

What Mike didn't know was that a day would come when Moobli's strength and courage would save his life for a second time.

For a long while, Mike had wanted to discover and photograph a family of eagles. One day, after a long search, he at last spotted a nest, an eyrie, just below the steep, craggy edge of a cliff. Commanding Moobli to stay, he climbed over. Then, to his horror, he lost his footing and slipped. As he fell, he managed to grab a tussock of grass. He hung there, motionless and frightened, knowing that only a clump of vegetation hung between him and certain death.

Then Mike glanced up to see Moobli staring at him from over the edge as if to say *what are you doing down there?*

'Moobli!' Mike gasped. 'Come here. Pull!'

Moobli knew exactly what *pull* meant. He had played games pulling at sticks with his master many times but when he heard the desperate tone of Mike's voice he knew instantly that this was no game. Mike tried to stay calm. When you live in the wilderness you get used to dangerous situations. But he knew if his dog didn't react rapidly he would soon be plunging to his death.

Mike needn't have worried. As he managed to slightly raise his arm Moobli moved forward and grabbed the sleeve of his jacket. He dug his hind claws into the peaty turf and heaved. He was so strong that Mike hardly even needed to use his own arm and leg muscles to pull himself back over the edge. As Moobli hauled him over the lip of the crag he knew the dog had saved his life a second time. If it hadn't been for his beloved dog, he would be dead.

On bitter winter nights, when the snow was deep and an icy wind would moan around the cottage, Moobli, his coat grown thick against the cold, would sit at Mike's feet while he tapped away on his typewriter. If Mike had made a list of all the wonderful things his dog did, it would have taken up several sheets of paper. He had asked a lot of his friend, more than most people could ever ask. He had endured the wild dangers of their treks together in all winds and weathers without complaint. He had willingly set his mind to any task Mike set him. He was more of a companion, a friend, a helper and protector than any human being could ever have been.

Moobli lived with Mike in their little cottage for almost nine years. During that time, Mike was unable to imagine life without him. Then, one day, he noticed that Moobli had started to limp after a long run in the woods. The dog would become stiff after a night's sleep and could hardly get up from his blanket. The condition became worse and it was with a sinking heart that Mike took him to see the vet. The vet confirmed that Moobli had a disease of the bones in his hind legs and although medication would help, the dog would never walk properly again, Mike was broken hearted but as time went by, he could see that although Moobli tried desperately to overcome his illness, he was in constant pain. Sadly Mike knew it was time for him to part with his faithful friend. After Moobli had been gently put to sleep and Mike had buried him on a hill overlooking the land the dog had loved so much, he believed that he could never stay on in the wilderness without him.

It was to be years before Mike Tomkies could write about his beloved dog. Later, though, he found the courage to begin a book about his life. He wanted other people to know what a wonderful animal Moobli had been and how his strength, his loyalty and his intelligence had made him a true wilderness dog.

BOTHIE
the Terrier who boldly went where no Dog had gone before

If you were going on a polar expedition and you needed something to cheer you up when you felt cold and lonely, what would you choose? The answer for gallant explorers, Ranulph and Ginny Fiennes, was Bothie, the Jack Russell terrier.

Ranulph and Ginny first set eyes on Bothie when he was only four weeks old. Even then, really too young to have been taken from his mother, the furry white sausage with brown patches over both eyes, showed an independence and cheekiness that was to keep up everyone's morale during their planned expedition to both the South and North Poles.

In spite of looking like a little white teddy bear, they soon learned Bothie was a bit of a handful. First, he refused to be housetrained, second, he ate people's shoes, third he hated going for walks. By the time the expedition was ready to set out, Bothie was two years old and still full of mischief. He was well prepared for the journey: little red polar jacket with ear covers, boots to keep his paws from getting frostbite. He was ready for anything.

What the little dog didn't know, though, was that his master and mistress were going to have to set off without him. The first leg of their epic journey was to take them by sea to South Africa. Bothie was to follow three months later by air.

The terrier must have wondered what was going on when he was shut in a small box and put in the hold of a gigantic jumbo jet, then placed in the back of a car for a long and hot journey across a strange land. But he took it all in his stride and he was over the moon when at the end of these puzzling events Ranulph and Ginny were waiting, anxious to be reunited with their beloved dog.

Bothie was soon to have another exciting experience for his journey was to continue by ship. On board he explored this strange new world that moved about under his paws. Then he decided that if he really had to do all this travelling then the best thing to do was make friends with the cook. A dog who never went hungry was a happy dog indeed.

But when the ship hit a storm, Bothie forgot all about food. He had refused to take his sea-sickness pills and lay on the floor moaning and groaning until it was over. Later, when the seas were calm again, Bothie was allowed up on deck. There he discovered lots of exciting things. For a start, there were seagulls to bark at when they dared to fly over the ship. He could play ball and throw his squeaky frog around and he could generally annoy everyone and have a great time. Life at sea, Bothie decided, wasn't that bad after all.

To keep Bothie secure, he wore a safety harness at all times. His owners knew they couldn't bear it if he fell overboard. He soon got used to the rough seas and ran about the deck whatever the weather. Bothie's cheeky face and boundless energy kept everyone amused during their long days at sea.

A few weeks later, Bothie arrived in the strangest land he had ever seen. Great ice cliffs loomed up in

front of the ship. There were strange smells. Seals, penguins . . . he simply couldn't wait to chase them. Soon after that Bothie became the first terrier ever to set paw on the biggest, whitest continent in the world. Antarctica.

The bitter temperatures made Bothie shiver and Ginny soon wrapped him in his thick, red polar jacket. She put his boots on too but he hated them. He growled and tore at them until they fell off. Terriers didn't wear boots. How could you chase things with boots on? He was carried down a long ladder to set paw on the ice. He looked around the endless stretch of white as if to say – look out everyone, Bothie of Antarctica has arrived!

During the eight months that the four members of the expedition team spent in a base camp hut on the ice, Bothie grew his own thick, cosy fur coat. This and his special high-fat diet kept him warm during the long, dark, bitter days. Ranulph and the rest of the team had gone on their trek across the continent to the Pole. Bothie and the others would join them later.

An Antarctic winter has no hours of daylight and during that time Bothie's antics kept up the spirits of Ginny and the others. With Bothie to look after and play with there was never a dull moment, night or day and while they waited anxiously to hear that Ranulph had arrived safely at the South Pole the little dog seemed a symbol of sunny days, a reason to get up in the morning. And when they did finally hear that the others had reached their goal, Ginny and Bothie set off in a plane to meet them. There is a permanent American base at the South Pole and there Bothie and the others spent the best Christmas ever.

Little did Bothie know that he wasn't destined to return to England for many more months but would be setting off on more exciting adventures. This time he would be heading for the *North* Pole. He must have given a sigh when he first heard the news. It had been a long time since he had seen any green grass or any other Jack Russells to make friends with, or even a lamppost to sniff.

Worse was to come for the intrepid terrier. He endured intense heat crossing the equator, then bitter winds blowing in from the approaching ice cap. Bothie was very annoyed when the ship taking them on the first leg of their journey south stopped at a New Zealand nature reserve and he wasn't allowed ashore. He stood on the deck while the others disembarked, whining miserably. It just wasn't fair.

Bothie wasn't allowed into Australia either although there, people came to see him. His fame as a daring and fearless explorer had spread. Children brought him presents – bones and toys – and the Jack Russell Club of Australia sent him a good luck message from all the Australian terriers. Best of all, Ginny brought aboard a sack of earth and straw and he rolled in it giving little barks of pleasure. Not quite like the green grass of home but better than nothing.

While the ship was docked, Ranulph and Ginny set up an exhibition about their adventures on the quayside and thousands of people came to see it. They wanted to see Bothie too and he paraded up and down the decks proudly, keeping an eye open for any lady Jack Russells he might be able to impress.

The next part of the voyage was hot: blazing sun, day after day. Bothie lay on the deck panting and irritable. He often wished they were back in that great, ice world with its white mountains and endless stretches of cold snow. He cheered up, though, when his master and mistress attached his harness to a long rope and he was allowed to swim in the sea to cool down. Ginny knew she would never forget the sight of her beloved little dog splashing around in the Pacific ocean.

When the ship reached America, to Bothie's relief, he *was* at last allowed ashore. The grass felt strange after the hard, wobbly decks of the ship.

There were to be lots more times when he would be able to run on dry land, for while Ranulph and the team continued their journey north, Bothie was to travel with Ginny by Land Rover up through Canada, on through the gold rush country of the Yukon then on to the North West Territories, all the time heading for the exciting dog adventures to be found at the northernmost tip of the planet. The North Pole!

By now, Bothie was a seasoned traveller. He had been on planes and ships, helicopters, sleds and skidoos. He'd done more exciting things in his short life than most dogs would ever do. He had met seals and penguins and huge sea birds, even a moose when he was playing ball with Ginny in a Canadian forest. He had heard the ghost-echo of his own voice bouncing back at him from caves of ice and had boldly explored cracks and crevices where no dog had gone before.

This final journey over mountains, across rivers and through mining camps was full of excitement too. Not only was Bothie soon to be reunited with his master, there was to be a new challenge for him. And a new friend. At their destination of Tuktoyaktuk, Bothie was to meet gophers, the little ground squirrels whose main aim in life seemed to be teasing the little terrier. He chased them for hours but he never caught one. To his annoyance, they always seemed to find a hole to pop down just as they were within snapping distance of his terrier teeth. There were other things there to annoy him too. Mosquitoes by the thousand. They drove him mad, although a soothing swim in Ginny's bath soon made him feel a lot better. There were also wolves that haunted the edges of the camp. Bothie barked at them bravely but was wise enough to keep his distance.

But all these minor irritations were forgotten because it was there at Tuktoyaktuk that Bothie fell in love with a tiny black Newfoundland puppy. Ginny fell in love with her too and she soon became a new member of the expedition. From now on there were to be two polar dogs – Bothie and Blackdog as she was named.

At Tuktoyaktuk, Ginny and Bothie waited anxiously for news of Ranulph and the rest of the team. Then at last came the message they had been waiting for. They had safely reached the North Pole. There had been many dangers to overcome including a fire in which they had lost a lot of their equipment. Waiting at the base, Ginny knew that if it hadn't been for Bothie and Blackdog she might have gone mad. And when the news of her husband's safe arrival did at last come she was ecstatic. She threw Bothie up in the air, caught him and gave him a huge cuddle. At first he was indignant. This was no way to treat a polar dog. But then he realised what a great event it was. His master and the others were the first men in the world to reach both Poles over the surface of the Earth. Bothie made up his mind there and then. *They* might be the first *men*, but he was going to be the first dog!

Bothie's dream came true when he and Ginny went by plane to meet Ranulph at the Pole. As he scrambled down the steps Bothie became the first dog in history to put four paws at both the South and North Poles.

After his final triumph, Bothie had to fly with

Blackdog back to England to stay in quarantine kennels while the expedition team stayed behind to clear up. When the dogs arrived home there was an army of photographers to meet them. Bothie was a hero and all the newspapers ran stories about his adventures. He took it all in his short stride. After all, Jack Russells *never* let fame go to their heads.

When they had been in the kennels for three months Bothie's favourite helper brought a newspaper in for him to look at. The expedition ship had docked and a week later two people arrived to cuddle him. He knew *exactly* who they were but decided to sulk as a punishment for leaving him so long. But when Ranulph produced Bothie's favourite rubber ball he gave in. He covered them both with kisses and his tail wagged so hard it almost fell off.

Three months later the dogs were allowed home. Ranulph and Ginny held a big party to celebrate. Friends turned up with presents galore. After that there were more photographs, and special pictures taken of him in his red polar jacket. Bothie appeared on TV and gave lots of interviews to the press. He was chosen as 'Pet of the Year' and presented with a medal at a special dinner in his honour.

Bothie accepted all the adoration like a star. After all, weren't Jack Russells famous for their bravery and fortitude? He decided that Ranulph and Ginny must have known that when they decided that he should be the dog to accompany them on the longest walkies ever. What's more, hadn't he got a gold medal to prove it?

GELERT
the Hound who gave his Life for a Prince

If you lived long ago in Beddgelert, a village in North Wales which lies at the foot of Moel Hebog with the towering Mount Snowdon as a backdrop, you might be invited to a *Nosweithiau Llawen* which in Welsh means 'a pleasant evening'. These pleasant evenings had been held since anyone could remember. They were a time when, on a cold, dark winter's night, friends would gather in someone's house for supper, often round a great, peat-burning fire. When the food had been eaten and Welsh songs had been sung it would be time for the ancient stories to be told. These stories had been handed down from generation to generation and the one that most people wanted to hear over and over again was the story of Gelert, the faithful deerhound who gave his life for a prince.

Gelert lived in the region over seven hundred years ago with his master Llewelyn ap Iorwerth. Llewelyn was nicknamed 'the Great' and is probably one of the most famous princes in ancient Welsh history.

These were very troubled times. The princes of North Wales were constantly under attack from the Marcher Lords of South Wales or English barons who hated their own King John, Llewelyn's father-in-law, and were seeking to spread their wealth into the Welsh territories. As well as having to contend with constant battles and sieges, Llewelyn had a large, hot-headed family who were always jealous of one another and plotting some kind of wrongdoing or other. Llewelyn was always under stress, whether it was from his family or his rivals from the southern marches. These were barbaric and dangerous times for princes and peasants alike.

When he wasn't fighting off his enemies or resisting attempts to dislodge him from his position of Lord of the Northern Marches, Llewelyn loved hunting. Hunting was his way of unwinding after a hard time keeping his lands and property out of the hands of his enemies, dealing with peasants' complaints and overseeing the upkeep of his farms. And when Llewelyn went hunting nothing gave him greater pleasure than riding through the thick forests and across the green valleys with his beloved deerhound by his side. The hound was the best hunting dog Llewelyn had ever owned. In fact, the dog was more than that. Whereas the other castle dogs roamed freely, coming and going as they wished, begging scraps from the kitchen and waiting for bones thrown from the huge dining table in the great hall, Gelert had a place of honour beside his master's chair. He was more than a working dog, he was his master's beloved companion.

Gelert had been a gift from Llewelyn's father-in-law and seemed to the prince a symbol of King John of England's affection. In those days it was a very good idea to have powerful friends who would send their armies to help you if you needed them. Gelert's presence reminded Llewelyn of this. As for the deerhound himself, he wanted nothing more than to be beside his master whether it was roaming the hills and valleys he loved so much, or running swiftly in front of his horse on one of their hunting expeditions. Gelert was tall and long-legged with a long, shaggy coat that kept him warm in the bitter Welsh winters. He had a keen nose and was so fleet-footed no other dog could keep up with him. He was also wise and cunning and a clever fighter which made him top of the assorted pack of castle dogs. Wolfhounds, spaniels, terriers, mastiffs, they all knew their place and kept well out of Gelert's way. Llewelyn was fond of the other dogs but Gelert was his favourite and always would be. He would trust him with his life.

One particular day, Llewelyn was in a bad mood.

He was well known for his irritable temper and when the servants heard him shouting they cringed. Many of them had been given a good beating for doing no more than forgetting to bow or not having the prince's horse quite ready when he suddenly took it into his head to go out.

This day, though, Llewelyn had a good reason to feel upset. His wife had gone to England to visit her father and he was missing her. More than that, she had left their baby son in his care and he was torn between his wish to go hunting and wanting to stay behind to look after the child. The tiny prince was too precious to be left in the care of servants but it was only when he was out hunting that

Llewelyn managed to forget the stresses and strains of everyday life and that week had been worse than most. The thick forests and green valleys, the towering presence of Snowdon seemed to call to him. There he could shrug off his troubles, especially if he had the fleet-footed Gelert running with him.

Llewelyn decided he *had* to go out or else he would go mad. He had to escape. There was only one thing holding him back. Who would look after the child while he was gone? Then he had an idea. He would leave Gelert to guard the cradle. He knew the faithful hound would protect the prince with his life. No harm would come to the child all the time Gelert was by his side. He called Gelert and took him up to the nursery and ordered him to 'stay'. The dog looked at him, puzzled, but lay down quietly beside the sleeping prince just as he had been commanded to do.

That day, Llewelyn chose a young mastiff to go with him and Gelert watched from the nursery window as men, horses and dogs set off. It was a bright morning, the dew sparkling in the sunlight. The sound of horses' hooves, the clatter of the hunting party, the barking of the dogs echoed through the early morning air. Gelert must have wished with all of his brave heart that he could go with them. There had been tales of a pack of wolves haunting the area and his job was to protect his master from such dangers. But today he had been ordered to do another task, today he had to protect someone who couldn't even begin to look after himself – the prince's baby son.

Gelert turned from the window and gazed at the sleeping infant. Then he lay down beside him on the wolfskin rug, his nose between his paws. With one ear cocked for danger, he drifted off to sleep.

Out in the forest, Llewelyn and his men kept their eyes open for wolves. A wolf hunt would make an exciting change even though the castle cook would be expecting venison to roast for supper and wouldn't be at all pleased to be presented with a dead wolf or two. The young mastiff the prince had chosen in Gelert's place was shaping up well. He wasn't nearly as fast as Llewelyn's beloved deerhound, or as intelligent, but for today, he would do.

Llewelyn thought about Gelert, faithfully guarding his baby son and felt contented that he had made a good decision to leave the dog behind.

Then, suddenly Llewelyn remembered something. He had been in such a rush to leave he had forgotten to feed the dog. He promised himself he would give Gelert an extra large, meaty bone when he got back, just to say he was sorry. The prince smiled to himself. His wife would be pleased when she got home and found the child had been so well looked after in her absence.

The day's hunt turned out well and it was late afternoon when men, horses and dogs made their way wearily home. The setting sun cast a rosy glow over the castle walls as the party clattered into the yard. Llewelyn had been pleased with the mastiff's performance. There had been no sign of any wolves but the dog had brought down a young deer. He would make a good hunting dog although he would never match Gelert. The prince was anxious to see his dog. He dismounted, ordered the dogs to be fed, threw the reins to his groom and strode across the courtyard. As he went indoors he heard Gelert barking his welcome and the dog came hurtling down the stone stairway to greet his master. He jumped up at the prince. Llewelyn frowned. Something was wrong. Hadn't he ordered Gelert not to leave the nursery until he was told he could do so? It wasn't at all like the dog to disobey an order. But Llewelyn was so pleased to see his hound he forgave him straight away.

It was then that Llewelyn noticed that his dog's coat was smeared with blood. He could smell it too. That hard, bitter iron smell of freshly spilled blood. He had smelled the same smell earlier when the mastiff had brought down the deer. His heart turned in horror. Gelert had been in the nursery all day. Where on earth could the bloodstains have come from?

Llewelyn took hold of the excited animal to get a closer look. His heart turned with terror again at what he saw. Gelert's teeth were red with blood. It was dripping from his open, panting mouth.

Llewelyn's men had followed him indoors and were standing in a group, muttering to themselves. Something dreadful had happened in their absence and none of them wanted to get the blame for it.

Llewelyn suddenly sprung into action. He pushed the dog away and rushed up the winding, stone stairs, his heart beating in terror. He could think of only one thing. His son.

When he reached the doorway to the nursery, Llewelyn flung aside the curtain that covered the entrance and hurtled inside. A scene more terrible than he could ever have imagined met his eyes. The child's cradle was lying on its side, empty. The covers had been dragged out and lay in a bloodstained heap on the floor. The wolfskin rug was stained with blood and gore. In the corner, the small bed in which his wife slept if the baby was fretful, had been dragged sideways. The blankets lay in a heap. They were smeared with blood too, as were the wall hangings and the curtains. The smell had spread throughout the room and it almost made him ill.

Gelert had rushed up the stairs with his master and stood panting by his side. His jaws still dripped with blood. He growled softly, menacingly, deep in his throat. Llewelyn turned on him in blind fury. The dog had been so hungry he had killed and eaten the young prince. Llewelyn aimed a kick at the surprised animal then grabbed the hunting knife from his belt and stabbed Gelert through the heart.

The dog's eyes were wide with surprise and hurt as he gave his master one feeble last lick and sank to the floor, dead.

The prince knelt by his side, weeping. Both his son and his beloved dog had perished. It was too much to bear.

It was then that Llewelyn heard a faint sound. He lifted his face from his hands. Had he imagined it? Then it came again. The soft sound of a baby's cry.

Llewelyn crawled across the bloodstained floor and lifted the corner of the cradle covers. There, underneath, was his son. Unharmed. The baby smiled when he saw his father and raised his arms to be picked up. Lewelyn lifted him from the floor and held him close. His son was safe – he could hardly believe it.

When Llewelyn's eyes cleared they fell on the body of Gelert. He handed the baby to one of the servants and went to kneel beside his dog. He had killed him in a fit of rage and fear without even stopping to find out what had really happened.

Then, out of the corner of his eye, the prince spotted something else. Beneath the small bed lay the body of a huge, grey wolf. It was dead, its throat torn out by Llewelyn's faithful Gelert as it entered the room to slaughter the baby prince.

Too overcome with guilt and sorrow even to speak, Llewelyn picked up the limp body of his brave dog. He noticed then the terrible wounds on the dog's body. Gelert had been gravely injured as he fought the wolf. Llewelyn knew he would never forgive himself as long as he lived.

Llewelyn carried Gelert through the gates of the silent castle and took him beyond the walls. He wanted to lay his dog to rest where he could be close to the forests, valleys and mountains that he had loved so much. He dug Gelert's grave with his own bare hands and buried him, weeping all the time and at last kneeling to beg the dog's forgiveness for the terrible thing he had done. He marked the grave and hoped that everyone who passed that way would forever remember the devoted and courageous dog who had saved the life of the son of Llewelyn ap Iorwerth.

Many centuries later, a man named David Pritchard came to live in the area where the ancient castle had once stood. He knew the famous story of Gelert and his heroic deed but the place where the dog had been buried had been lost many, many years before. David decided to put up a cairn of stones to honour the brave animal.

That memorial is still there today and the village takes its name from the story – Beddgelert, the grave of Gelert and just as Llewelyn had hoped, all who now pass that way remember the faithful deerhound and the tale itself is probably the best loved story of a devoted dog in the whole world.

MICKY
the Digger Dog

The Perks family had two dogs. One of them, Micky, a black and white rough coated Jack Russell, belonged to Bill and Jean who lived in Yorkshire. The other dog, Percy, a chihuahua, belonged to their daughter, Christine, who lived nearby with her small son, Alex. Although the Perks considered both the animals as *family* pets, the dogs obviously had other ideas. They hated one another. It was very strange. Both dogs were given the same amount of attention, they both probably thought of Bill, Jean, Christine and Alex as their own family but they just could not hit it off.

Whatever the reason was, whenever the dogs got together they scrapped. These quarrels were never serious and made the family laugh. The frantic growling and baring of teeth never really amounted to anything and the family had lots of fun watching them sort out their differences. Micky and Percy would argue as to who was allowed in the kitchen, who was allowed on Bill or Jean's lap, who had the best place in front of the fire. Neither dog ever particularly seemed to be the winner. Sometimes Micky would back down, sometimes Percy. Maybe they just enjoyed fighting? The family decided that it wasn't so much that they hated one another, they were just jealous in case one got more attention than the other. And however hard the family tried to divide their love equally between the two dogs – things never changed.

One day, Christine decided to pay one of her many visits to her parents. She dressed Alex, put him in his buggy and set off with Percy trotting along beside them. He was excited at the thought of going out. He was probably even looking forward to seeing his old enemy, Micky. He bounded along at the end of his lead, full of the joys of spring.

Bill and Jean were delighted to see Christine and Alex . . . and Percy, of course. They made their usual fuss of the little dog, making sure they made a fuss of Micky too. As usual, Micky had barked and growled fiercely when Percy appeared in the house. Percy had growled back, challenging Micky to their usual duel. When all this had died down, the family went into the front room while Jean went into the kitchen to make tea.

As they sat talking and playing with Alex and catching up on the news, Christine suddenly noticed Percy wasn't in the room with them. With horror, she remembered she had left the back door open intending to bring the buggy inside in case it rained. Her parents' home was on a busy main road and her heart thudded with fear as she ran outside to look for the little dog. Jean had run upstairs to see if he was in any of the bedrooms and Bill was calling for Percy and searching in the other downstairs rooms.

As she ran round to the front of the house, Christine saw a car had stopped in the centre of the road. Her heart turned over. There was a woman bending over something lying in the road. She was crying noisily.

Christine's worse fears were realised as she ran out of the garden gate. Percy was lying in the road, not moving. The woman driver of the car was kneeling beside him, tears streaming down her face. As Christine knelt beside her she noticed blood oozing from poor Percy's mouth and from a cut under his chin. He had run out straight in front of the vehicle and there had been no chance for the driver to slam on her brakes and avoid him. 'I'm so sorry,' she sobbed to Christine. 'There was absolutely nothing I could do.'

By now, Bill and Jean had arrived on the scene. They all wept bitterly as Bill picked up the limp body of the little dog and carried him gently back into the house. They got his blanket and laid him on the kitchen table. Micky stared up at everyone wondering what was going on. Why was his old enemy lying so still? Why couldn't he jump off the table so Micky could try to bite him?

Jean and Christine sobbed as Bill examined Percy. He could find no heartbeat at all. Sadly he looked at his wife and daughter. They were both so upset he decided the kindest thing to do would be to bury Percy as quickly as possible. Jean and Christine agreed. The best place to put him would be in the garden. After all, in spite of his fights with Micky, little Percy had loved visiting Bill and Jean's house.

By now it was raining and Micky watched as Bill put on his wellington boots. Something told the little terrier that they wouldn't be going out for a walk that day. He followed Bill as he went to the shed to fetch a spade and began to dig a hole at the end of the garden. When the hole was about half a metre deep Bill decided it would do. There weren't any foxes or badgers around that would be likely to dig Percy up. Jean had found a paper sack and they gently placed the little dog's body inside. Jean, Christine, Alex and Micky watched sadly as Bill put the sack into the hole and covered it with earth. Micky was still confused. Putting the chihuahua into a bag and burying him seemed a very strange thing to do.

After the terrible tragedy Christine and Alex couldn't face going home on their own so Jean went with them. It was a sad little trio that set off for Christine's house. In her bag was Percy's collar and lead. Life would seem very empty without the little dog they had all loved so much. Except for Micky, of course, although Christine had a sneaking feeling the terrier would miss Percy as much as anyone.

At Micky's house, Bill sat watching TV. His mind kept going back to Percy and he felt sad at the little dog's sudden and violent death. He put his hand down to stroke Micky. The Jack Russell seemed more precious than ever now Percy was gone.

As Bill put his hand down, he suddenly realised Micky wasn't there beside him. In fact, now he thought about it, he hadn't seen the terrier for quite a while. For a moment he froze. Surely the same thing hadn't happened again? Jean and Christine would never forgive him.

Bill was just getting up to go and search for him when Micky suddenly appeared. Bill gazed at him in horror. The terrier was covered in mud. What on earth had he been up to? Not only was Micky filthy but there was something wrong with him. He ran up and down the room: to the TV, round the armchair, behind the settee and out again. Bill began to get annoyed with him. Hadn't they had enough trouble for one day without the dog spreading mud all over the place? He realised the terrier must be wondering what had happened to his old adversary but that was no excuse for messing up the house. Jean would be furious.

When Micky jumped up at Bill and pawed at him, scrabbling at his knees, Bill got *really* annoyed. It was obvious Micky wanted to go out into the muddy garden again. Bill got up and shut the door firmly.

He'd got enough mess to clean up before Jean got home without Micky making it even worse. It was only later that the man realised the terrier had been desperately trying to tell him something in his own doggie way. But at the time Bill thought he was simply being naughty.

Much later in the evening, Jean came home. She hadn't got her front door key so she went round to the back. As she glanced sadly down to the place where Percy had been buried she saw a gruesome sight. Percy was lying on the garden path, the paper sack in shreds around him. Jean gazed in horror. Who or what could have done such a terrible thing as to dig up the little dog's dead body? Her daughter

and grandson would be more upset than ever when they learned what had happened. She ran indoors to tell Bill.

Bill was furious. He knew now how Micky had got covered in mud. He had dug his old enemy up!

Bill shouted at Micky as he got his coat and boots ready to go and re-bury the poor chihuahua. Micky, being a Jack Russell, didn't care a bit about being yelled at. He had something far more important on his mind. As Bill opened the back door, Micky tore outside. He dashed up to Percy and began frantically licking the poor animal. Micky whined deep in his throat as if he was begging Percy to wake up. Bill couldn't believe his eyes. He had always been led to believe that animals sensed when another had died. He couldn't think of a single reason for Micky's odd behaviour.

But as he got closer to Micky, everything suddenly became clear. As Bill bent down to shoo the terrier away he suddenly noticed something. Percy's chest was rising and falling feebly. The little dog was still breathing! Bill touched Percy's body. It was warm and beneath his fingertips he could feel a faint heartbeat. There was no doubt about it, the chihuahua was still alive!

All at once, Bill saw Micky's behaviour in a different light. All that pawing and whining had meant something. Micky had wanted Bill to go outside to show him he had dug Percy out of the ground and that his old enemy wasn't dead at all.

But how on earth had Micky known?

Bill didn't have time to stop and think about it. As he picked Percy up to take him indoors, he noticed the chihuahua's face was clean where Micky had been licking him. Later the family learned that it had probably been this that had helped Percy to stay alive. Micky's uncanny canine instinct had told him that Percy was breathing but that he *would* die soon if he wasn't dug up and brought out into the open air. Terriers are, by nature, digging dogs and can tell whether an invisible prey is alive or dead. Mountain and disaster rescue dogs can be trained to tell their handler whether a buried body is breathing or not. Micky's natural instinct to unearth things had been alerted and in this case it had saved another dog's life.

Jean was amazed to see her husband bringing Percy back indoors. She had imagined Bill would have had the grisly job of re-burying the chihuahua straight away. When Bill told her what had happened he bent to give Micky a hug. What a brilliant dog he had turned out to be! As they wrapped Percy up warmly Micky jumped up to see what was going on. He gave a bark. It looked as if Percy would live on to fight another day.

As Jean phoned Christine to tell her the good news, Bill rushed Percy to the vet. The little dog was still extremely poorly, hardly breathing at all. It proved very difficult to keep his body warm. The vet was amazed when he heard what had happened and promised to do everything he could to keep Percy alive.

For almost a week it was touch and go. Percy hovered on the brink of death. Christine visited him every day but all she could do was stand and gaze at his still body. He was breathing but in a coma. Everyone hoped he wouldn't have any brain damage but no-one would be able to tell until he woke up. Christine couldn't bear the thought of that. After all Percy had been through and Micky's heroic effort in saving his life – it would just be too much to bear.

Then, after five days, days that seemed the longest the family had ever known, Christine went to the vet's one morning and found Percy standing up and wagging his tail. She could hardly believe her eyes and cried all over again at her pet's miraculous recovery. Percy was still a little weak and wobbly but after spending another day at the surgery, she was allowed to take him home.

No-one could remember exactly how long Percy had been buried. But they guessed it must have been several hours. It seemed possible that the air trapped in the paper sack had been enough to sustain the little dog's shallow breathing. But one thing they were sure of was that if it hadn't been for Micky, the chihuahua would have eventually suffocated and no-one would ever have known that he had been buried alive.

The story of Micky's heroism soon spread and before long he was featured in the newspapers. One of them put him forward as Pet of the Year and he was presented with a gold medal for his bravery. He got letters from all over the country and gifts of money to buy himself and Percy presents.

And as for Percy? He was soon back to his old self again. He and Micky remained the best of enemies and carried on just as if nothing unusual had ever happened. When Percy visited Micky's house, the terrier still went for him in just the same old way. He would curl his lip and growl as if to say – 'OK, so I saved your life but that doesn't mean I like you so ther-r-r-re!'

BALTO

the Dog who kept on running and saved an Alaskan Town

If you were to visit New York's Central Park, an oasis of green in the centre of a huge, noisy city, you would soon come across a life-sized bronze statue of a dog. The statue is on a hill overlooking the park and even though it is made of metal, it is so life-like you can almost see the bravery and determination in the dog's eyes. The statue is of Balto, a courageous and intelligent Siberian husky who lived in Alaska over seventy years ago.

Balto became famous because he overcame many dangers as he led a sled dog team carrying vital medicine through the savage winter wilderness of Alaska to a town where the people had been stricken by a deadly disease.

The famous event took place in 1925. This decade

saw the dawn of the age of the aeroplane and travel across the states of North America and Canada was becoming easier. Goods and supplies that had previously taken a long time to travel during the wintertime could now be flown to the remoter regions of the North where there were few road or rail connections.

But the winter of 1925 was a very severe one and no planes could fly through the dense blizzards that swept the landscape during January and February. The weather was so bad that all the roads were blocked by snowdrifts and steam trains didn't reach as far as a small town called Nome where a serious diphtheria epidemic had broken out. The disease could only be treated with a special serum to fight the bacteria and the nearest stock of this was in Anchorage on the other side of Alaska. There was only one way that the life saving medicine could reach Nome – by dog sled. For centuries, people in Siberia have relied on dog teams to ferry goods and people to and fro and this mode of transport had proved ideal for the Alaskan people. Now in this harsh winter, it was all they had.

Today, people are vaccinated against diphtheria but in those days it could prove fatal. In this outbreak, many had already died. It was a desperate situation. If the serum didn't get through, everyone in the town might perish.

When the people of Nome realised how desperate their situation was, they sent out an urgent message by telegraph to Anchorage, five hundred kilometres away. 'Please help us or else we shall die!'

A few years before this happened, amongst a litter of Siberian husky puppies, one in particular might have caught your eye. He was a black dog with soft, intelligent eyes. Even though he was gentle, he didn't allow the other puppies to push him around. And although his owners didn't know it, this young dog was a born leader. He was to become Balto, the lead dog of the sled team that saved many lives by bringing the serum to the stricken people of Nome.

When Anchorage got the urgent message from the Nome telegraph office everyone sprung into action. They knew that speed was vital. The serum was packed quickly into boxes and put on a train heading for Nenana, the small town at the end of the line. The train ploughed through terrible conditions. At times the driver thought they wouldn't make it but at last they reached their destination. The town was over three hundred kilometres from Nome and from then on, a relay of dog sleds would take over.

Word had gone on ahead and dog teams were waiting. As the train pulled into the station through a blinding snow storm they barked excitedly. Siberian huskies love pulling sleds. More than this, they love snow and for them, this was going to be an adventure. The thought of fighting a battle with a raging storm didn't worry them at all.

The serum was loaded straight on to the waiting

sled and the first team set off, their leader setting the pace. They pushed north, fighting the icy winds, through the blizzards and snowdrifts that almost halted them. The musher, the person who guides the dogs, could hardly see for snow hitting his face like needles. But he knew they had to press on – hundreds, maybe thousands of lives were at stake.

When they reached the first small town, a fresh team was waiting. While the first team recovered, the new ones were soon put in harness, setting off through the storm for the next stopping place. There was no let up in the snow as the musher cracked his whip and the lead dog leapt forward. At first they were fresh and eager and made good progress. But as the storm worsened they grew weary and were ready to give up. Their musher urged them forward until at last they staggered into a little town where a new team waited.

The storm didn't abate as the third team set off. In spite of the conditions they too made good progress at first. They managed to keep to the trail, the musher urging them onward. But the going got harder and after a few hours the dogs were getting worn out. At last they reached Bluff, the next small town on the route to Nome. Dogs and musher were frozen and weary, ready to collapse with fatigue. Although they had been on the trail for hours they had covered only fifteen kilometres. There were another forty kilometres to go before a team reached Nome. In this weather, it could take them many days.

As the team struggled wearily into town, another team was waiting anxiously. The dogs barked with excitement as they spotted the weary huskies coming towards them. They were impatient to be off. But the musher advised against going on. Outside it was thirty degrees below freezing, the wind was screeching through the air and snowdrifts were piling higher and higher with every minute that passed. Visibility was almost nil and it would take a miracle dog to find the trail.

'You'll never make it,' he gasped to the new team's musher, Gunnar Kasson. 'My dogs almost froze to death. Yours will do the same.'

But what the man didn't know was that the lead dog of Mr Kasson's team was Balto.

Balto didn't belong to Gunnar Kasson. He was owned by a man named Leonard Seppala. Mr Seppala had been one of the first people to introduce Siberian huskies as working dogs in America. He and his dog teams had already covered some of the relay to Nome. With his lead dog, Togo, he had crossed the frozen Norton Bay and had depended upon Togo's sense of direction in the blinding snow. Mr Seppala had allowed Mr Kasson to use Balto. He knew if any dog could take the sled team safely on this next-to-last stage of the journey to Nome, it would be him.

As the previous musher and his dogs recovered

from their ordeal, Balto and the new team set off through the storm. Balto didn't know how far he was required to go. All he knew was that his master had ordered him to set off in the face of the blizzard and that the other dogs were relying on him. Many Siberian huskies are half-wild and difficult to train, but Balto was different. He had a more gentle nature and he trusted his master and was quick to obey commands. He was intelligent and sensitive and had a great instinct for danger. Mr Kasson knew this and that was why, on that bitter, blinding day, he was glad to have Balto to lead the other dogs into the wilderness.

What neither Balto, *nor* Mr Kasson knew, though, was that they were to face more dangers than they could ever have imagined.

As they set off for the thirty kilometre trek to a town called Safety where the next and final team would be waiting, Mr Kasson's heart sank. A musher is there to guide and encourage his dogs and they relied on him to show them the way forward. Without him, they might try to scatter in all directions, tangling harnesses and pulling against one another instead of hauling the heavily loaded sled. Mr Kasson knew this was going to be the hardest journey he was ever to make.

First of all, the blizzard was so thick he couldn't even see his dogs, let alone guide them. More than once he thanked his lucky stars Balto was in front. He knew the big, black dog could smell the trail.

He knew he would stay on it. As the husky leapt forward Mr Kasson knew he would have to trust him completely. He cracked his whip above the dogs' heads calling, 'Mush!', 'Get going!' as they moved onwards, running eagerly forward into the teeth of the storm.

The first part of the trail from Bluff to Safety was across sea ice. This ice is usually packed hard and it is a good surface for the dogs to run on. Mr Kasson thought they would make good time. But he soon found out he was wrong. The gale was blowing so hard that waves had formed beneath the ice. It was heaving up and down like a roller coaster. The dogs were frightened as they felt it move beneath their paws. It was like being on the deck of a ship in a storm-tossed sea. Siberian huskies are usually very sure footed but this time they skipped and skidded, their legs going in all directions. The sled was thrown off balance, tripping and weaving over the moving, bumpy ice. It toppled over so many times Mr Kasson almost gave up and turned back to Bluff. The dogs were more scared than ever, yipping and snapping at one another as he fought to right the upturned sled. Balto barked at them as if to say, 'Keep calm – he's doing his best.' And when the squabbling dogs saw Balto was standing patiently and quietly, they calmed down and waited until the sled was on its runners again and ready to go forward.

It seemed to Balto that they had been travelling

for hours. He was tired and freezing cold. His legs ached and his paws were red and raw from the sharp needles of ice that pierced his pads. He desperately wanted to stop and rest but knew that he couldn't. His master kept pushing him forward. He sensed the urgency of their mission. This wasn't an ordinary sled run: it was a matter of life or death.

Balto and the team were getting close to the edge of the sea ice when the dog suddenly heard a sound that made his blood run cold and set his heart pounding with fear. His master hadn't heard it, he was still driving the team forward in a straight line heading for the welcome firmness of solid ground. Mr Kasson shouted as Balto skidded to a halt and refused to go any further. Then, when he did set off again the dog swerved in another direction. Balto couldn't have done anything else. The noise he had heard was the cracking of the ice splitting apart. The cold water, tossed into a frenzy by the gale would soon seep through the cracks. If Balto hadn't changed course, the team, the sled and Mr Kasson would have plunged into the icy sea. If this happened they would never get out. They and their precious cargo would be lost for ever.

Then Mr Kasson heard the terrible sound too and realised what Balto was up to. He let him find his own way across the ice, silently praying it would be the right one. The dog was heading out to sea, running swiftly, barking now and then as if to encourage and urge the others forward. Then, to Mr Kasson's relief Balto turned north again to pick up the trail that would lead to the town of Safety, then eventually on to Nome. He heaved a sigh. For now, the danger was past. Once again they were heading for the place where a new team would be waiting to ferry the serum on the last leg of the journey. They should be there soon.

By now Balto and the other dogs were exhausted. They had been running for well over twelve hours. Balto could feel the others dragging on the traces. But he knew they had to go on. He barked. It was as if he was saying, 'Come on, we're almost there.' His instincts told him if they stopped to rest they would freeze to death.

It was hours later that Mr Kasson realised they must have missed Safety altogether. The journey had taken too long. They should have arrived hours ago. The people waiting there would think they had perished in the storm. But there was no turning back, they would have to carry on and head right on to Nome. It would mean that Balto and the relay team had to cover twice the distance that had been planned for them. Mr Kasson gritted his teeth and urged the dogs onward. Balto had led them this far, all he could hope for was that the dogs had the strength and courage to carry on.

The nightmare was to continue for another few hours. At the head of the team, Balto fought to see through the howling, needle sharp storm. They were all caked with frozen snow, their coats as stiff as cardboard. At the back of the sled, Mr Kasson looked like a snowman. Their pace was getting slower and slower. Mr Kasson doubted they would ever make it. He had visions of the dogs collapsing with exhaustion, the vital serum lost for ever in the snowy wilderness. Perhaps it would be found in the spring when the sun melted the snowdrifts. But by then it would be too late. The people of Nome would have been wiped out. It would turn into a ghost town as the disease killed off the inhabitants one by one.

At last, though, thanks to Balto's leadership and determination and the bravery of all the huskies, the sled made it to Nome. At dawn on the bitterly cold morning of February 2nd, Balto and his team struggled into the town. They had been running for twenty four hours. The residents of Nome were saved.

'You're our hero,' people cried as they lined up to collect the vital serum. But Mr Kasson shook his head.

'If it hadn't been for Balto,' he said, 'we would never have got through.'

After that, Balto became a national hero. Many newspaper stories and books were written about his epic journey. There were books written about him too and he became a symbol of the unique courage of all the huskies in the relay. Each dog had played a vital part in the desperate run to Nome, although it is the name of Balto that will always be remembered.

Two thirds of that heroic trek had followed a route called the Iditarod Trail. The name comes from a Native American word meaning 'far distant place'. This trail became a way to reach those remote towns in Alaska. It was full of swamps in the summer but in winter it was a major route for the dog sled teams that were used by most people at that time.

Today, a great sled race called the Iditarod is run every year from Anchorage to Nome. The race was inspired by the heroic run of Balto and the other huskies. It is watched by thousands of people, many of whom are descendants of those whose lives were saved by Balto, the brave dog who just simply kept on running.

JUDY
Dog of War

When HMS *Grasshopper* sailed for the Far East during the Second World War she had a very important member of the crew aboard, her canine mascot, Judy.

Judy, a pointer, was to play a very important part in the lives of the men who served in the British forces. In fact, many who were later to spend agonising months in the hands of the Japanese, vowed they could not have survived without her. The dog's intelligence and courage served as an inspiration to everyone she came into contact with. If she could survive, then so could they!

Judy had served with the Navy ever since she was a tiny puppy. She had already been the mascot of several other ships before she joined the crew of the *Grasshopper* and she had seen lots of war action. On HMS *Grasshopper* she was listed as an official member of the crew and had her own identity disc *'Judy – Mascot of HMS Grasshopper'*. She was as vital to the morale of the men and the smooth running of the ship as any other member of the crew.

It was December, 1941 and Britain had already been at war with Germany for over two years. Suddenly, and without the intelligence forces suspecting a thing, the Japanese airforce attacked Pearl Harbour, an important American base in the Pacific Ocean. This horrific assault forced Britain to go to war with Japan. British Naval forces struggled to stop this new enemy but the odds against them were overwhelming. No-one could halt the Japanese in their sinister advance towards India. One by one they captured strategic bases in Malaya and the, then called, East Indies. The war had entered a new stage.

When Singapore was invaded the *Grasshopper* was bombed by the Japanese air force. Many of the crew managed to escape the wreck but went through a traumatic time as they tried to reach Sumatra where they believed British warships were moored. Many of the men were injured and sick as they struggled by land and by sea to reach safety. Judy stayed with them. She suffered all the hardships that they were going through: near drowning, starvation, sickness, exhaustion. When the desperate men were eventually caught by the Japanese she was captured with them and taken to a prison camp.

Along with the men who had been on board

Grasshopper were thousands of other prisoners. They were all housed in ramshackle, ill-equipped huts. These camps were appalling places to be in. There was no fresh water, hardly any food and hundreds of men were crammed together into tiny spaces hardly even big enough for a few dozen. The tropical heat caused immense suffering to the men from the milder European climate. Sunstroke, sickness and disease were commonplace and hundreds died. A law made at the Geneva Convention in the last century sets out rules for the decent treatment of war prisoners but it seemed that few of the Japanese commanders had ever heard of them. The conditions in these camps needed strength, stamina and a determination to survive them. It seemed Judy had all of these qualities.

Eventually, Judy and a contingent of prisoners were sent to a camp in Medan, in northern Sumatra. All the men who had cared for the brave animal had fallen by the wayside. They were either dead or had been taken elsewhere. Judy was confused and upset. All she knew was that she must stay with these humans who spoke a language she could understand.

Among the remaining British contingent was an airman, Frank Williams. Frank was fond of dogs and Judy was to become his faithful friend.

When Judy first spotted Frank he was crouched in the corner of a squalid tin hut, staring miserably at a meagre tin cup of sticky rice. It was to be his only meal that day. Frank knew it would taste foul. He also knew if he didn't eat it he would starve. He suddenly realised he was being stared at and when he looked up he saw Judy, thin and ragged from her long journey. She was gazing at him intently. Although she had been allowed to stay with the British prisoners, no-one so far had thought of feeding her. All she could do was scavenge food wherever she could and often a couple of the rats that infested the camp was all she would have to eat for days on end.

When Frank saw the pitiful animal staring at him, his heart went out to her. Just as hers did to him. Both man and dog were hungry, frightened and exhausted. Already there was a bond between them.

As Frank looked at Judy her tail gave a sudden thump. Her wide, brown eyes seemed to be melting as he watched her. He scooped a morsel of rice into the palm of his hand and held it towards her. Judy didn't move. She had been shouted at and kicked so often since she was captured that she didn't trust anyone. She gave a little whine but her hackles were up and she was too wary to move.

Frank knew how to get a dog's trust. First he held his free hand out for her to sniff. He murmured soft words to the petrified animal. Then, as she finally allowed him to stroke her, she relaxed and leaned against his knees. Then she took the rice, licking every grain from his fingers. It was pretty horrible but obviously better than rat meat. As

Frank patted her she wagged her tail joyfully. At last she had found a friend. And so had Frank.

From then on the friendship between man and dog grew stronger each day. Judy came to see him the next day, then the day after, sharing Frank's pitiful rations as though they were a banquet. Soon, Frank had taught her to lie down, to sit and stay on command, to come to him or to make herself scarce. He knew the pointer's survival depended upon her keeping out of the guards' way. Almost without exception they hated her and would have killed her at the first opportunity. They saw how she brought comfort into the lives of Frank and the other prisoners and were determined to get rid of her.

Wisely, she avoided them. At night she would leave the camp although no-one knew where she went. In the morning she would reappear, often bringing gifts for Frank, flowers, once a dead rat. Even this made the men laugh. Her kindness reminded them of home. They would think of their houses, their families, their own dogs, the park where children could play safely. Judy's friendship gave them hope that one day they would see all these things once more.

Bringing presents for Frank often brought trouble down on Judy's head. Once she made a fool of the guards by depositing an imitation skull on Frank's bunk. The skull belonged to one of the prisoners who had used it for his medical studies before he was captured. The Japanese guards thought it was real and saw it as a symbol of death. The prisoners laughed when they ran from the hut in fear. But when the guards found out their mistake, they were very angry. They felt they had been made fools of and that it was Judy's fault. If Frank hadn't yelled at her to make herself scarce they would have killed her there and then. Frank *had* found the incident hilarious, but now he had second thoughts. If Judy was killed he didn't know if he would have the strength to carry on. He racked his brains to try to think of a way to protect her. But how? That was the problem.

Later, Frank came up with an idea. Why not make Judy the camp mascot? If she was an official member of the armed forces then she must be an official prisoner of war. 'Yes,' a friend of Frank's agreed. 'Then she'll be protected under the Geneva Convention just like us.' Some of the other men scoffed. They knew the guards had little respect for such rules. If they had, then their treatment of the prisoners wouldn't have been half so bad.

But Frank believed the idea would be better than nothing. They might be clutching at straws but he would do anything to keep Judy alive.

Again, Frank racked his brains but he couldn't think of a way to carry out his scheme. He felt desperate. Judy's days were numbered and if he didn't do something soon it might well be too late.

As it turned out, Judy herself found a solution. Frank and the other men noticed Judy was putting on weight. In spite of near-starvation she was managing to look well. Secretly, Frank thought she had other special friends who were sharing their rice with her. He didn't mind a bit. As long as she was there to give him the strength and courage he needed to survive then it was OK with him. Then the dog disappeared for a while and Frank feared his worst nightmare had come true. Judy had been shot and left to die in some filthy corner of the camp. He was heartbroken.

A week or so later, though, Judy reappeared. This time she had another gift for Frank – five roly-poly puppies who scampered after her as she came into the hut. They were amazingly fit and healthy for the conditions they had been born into. Frank was so proud of Judy and he and the other men spent hours of fun watching the youngsters roll and play in the dry dust of the camp. They seemed like a tonic to men starved of fun.

Then Frank had a brainwave. He saw the chance he had been waiting for and he could put the idea into practice right away.

It so happened that the camp commander had a lady friend. And the lady friend liked dogs. Frank had seen her making a fuss of Judy when she came on a visit. She always had a kind word for the dog who, surprisingly, seemed fond of her too.

One day, when Frank knew the commander was alone, he went to visit him. He was taking his life into his hands. If the commander was in a foul mood he could have Frank shot for his cheek. But that day Frank's luck held. He went into the commander's office with one of the puppies in his arms. The commander laughed when the little dog sat and stared at him, with its head on one side. 'He's charming,' he said to Frank in good English.

Frank told the commander the puppy was a present for his lady friend and, thankfully, the man was pleased. He would take the puppy to her and he knew she would be delighted. Frank heaved a sigh of relief. His plan had worked.

It was then that Frank asked if Judy could be made an official prisoner of war. Deep down, the Japanese commander was a kindly man and had a good sense of humour. If Judy had honoured his lady friend with the gift of a puppy then he would repay her kindness. There and then he scribbled an official note and handed it to Frank. Judy became *Prisoner 81A – Medan.*

Frank's success made him even more determined to protect the dog. He hadn't risked the fury of the commander for nothing.

Soon after that, though, conditions became even worse. The kindly commander was replaced and the new one hated dogs. When the men were moved to another camp, this time in Singapore, he ordered Judy to be left behind. He saw how fond they were of her and decided enough was enough. These men were prisoners of war and didn't deserve the privilege of keeping pets. Frank, though, had other ideas. He knew if Judy stayed she would be killed. He commanded her to stay out of sight until they were ready to leave. For thirty six hours she hid, then, just as the trucks were ready to go, Frank gave his special whistle. She ran out of her hiding place and hid in a rice sack that he held open for her. He slung it over his back and carried her into the lorry heading for the docks where they were to board a ship for the next stage of their journey.

The guards had been ordered to keep an eye out for the hated dog but not once did Judy move or make a sound that might give her away.

This wasn't the end of Judy's adventures. The ship was torpedoed and Frank lost her in the chaos that followed. After two hours in the sea, he was picked up by a tanker. Judy was nowhere to be seen. This time, Frank thought miserably, he would never see her again. He was taken to another camp but without Judy he lost the will to live. If he didn't have his beloved dog he might as well die.

Miraculously, though, Judy *had* survived. She had been hauled aboard a Chinese junk by Frank's friend. However, when they reached Singapore a shock awaited them. There on the quayside was the cruel commander who had ordered Judy to be left in the camp. Now, as Judy lay on the quay, soaked to the skin, shaking and close to death, he ordered her to be shot. Silently and helplessly the prisoners watched the Japanese guards raise their rifles. Their dear friend was to die and there was nothing they could do about it.

But Judy's luck hadn't run out. Another voice rang out. This time it was the commander who had taken the gift of the puppy. He shouted at the men to lower their guns. The dog was an official prisoner of war and must be respected. Thanks to the man's sense of honour, Judy was saved.

Two days later, Frank was to be reunited with his dog. He was lying on his bunk simply waiting to die when he heard a joyful bark and there stood his pal with Judy by his side. He couldn't believe his eyes. There and then he vowed he would never give up hope again.

That faith was rewarded as the prisoners managed

to keep Judy with them through more months of terrible conditions. She was by Frank's side when he was taken to work on the building of a railway through the jungle. Many times she warned the men of dangers from animals, insects and snakes. She risked her life defending them from attack. But her greatest gift to the men she loved was keeping up their spirits in some of the most dreadful conditions any human being has ever had to endure. Many times they decided that if the courageous dog could put up with such an existence, then so could they. And when the end of the war finally came Frank was determined to take Judy back to England. She had saved his life – he would keep her by his side for ever.

After their release, Frank and Judy waited for a ship to bring them home. 'No dogs on board' a sign said at the end of the gangway. Frank's heart sank. Then he remembered something. Judy was an ex-prisoner of war, she would go home like all the others who had survived.

So Frank smuggled Judy on board and brought her triumphantly home to Great Britain where she could live out the rest of her life in peace.

After her six months in quarantine Frank took the pointer home. Judy became a heroine. She was awarded the Dickin Medal – the highest award a dog can receive. She became an honoured member of the Returned British Prisoners Association and Frank received a medal from the

People's Dispensary for Sick Animals in recognition of his care and protection of Judy.

At home, by his fireside once more, Frank often thought of the puppies that Judy had left behind. He wondered if they remembered their mother, Judy, the brave and devoted dog of war.

CINDER
the Hero's Hero

Lorenzo Abundiz always wanted two things. The first was to be a firefighter and the second was to own Rottweilers.

Lorenzo's first ambition came true when he began his job as a firefighter with the Los Angeles Fire Department in California, USA. His second wish was fulfilled when he found himself the owner of not one, but two Rottweilers. One of the dogs, Cinder, was to save his life.

It was no coincidence that Lorenzo achieved his first ambition. From the very beginning it seemed he was destined to be a firefighter. When his mother gave birth to him he was delivered by a fireman and the house he lived in was next door to a fire station. As a boy he would watch the firefighters training and feel a sense of excitement when he heard the sirens and saw the fire engines race out of the building to fight fires all over the city. He saw how fit and strong you had to be to become a firefighter and made up his mind that when he was old enough he would join the service. He took up the sport of body building so he would be powerful enough and passed all his exams with flying colours.

When Lorenzo spent his first proud day as a raw recruit he didn't know it but in the course of his duty he was to become a hero. And it was one particular act of heroism that would lead him to Cinder.

One day, when Lorenzo and his fellow firefighters were called out to a fire at a factory they didn't know what to expect. When they got there, other firefighters were already on the scene and the building was an inferno. To Lorenzo's horror he learned that two firemen were trapped inside.

Without even taking the time to put on breathing apparatus, Lorenzo dived in. The precious minutes it would have taken to put on his oxygen kit might mean death to the trapped men. As he plunged into the burning building Lorenzo could hear the men shouting behind a huge collapsed wall partition. He knew that to rescue them he would have to lift it. All the hours he had spent in the gym improving his strength paid off as he heaved the barrier aside to free the desperate men.

For this heroic action, Lorenzo received the medal of valour from the California State Fireman's Association. He appeared on several television shows for his amazing feat of bravery. Lorenzo received something else, too. A gift from one of the grateful men he had rescued. A Rottweiler puppy – Cinder.

Right from the beginning, Lorenzo knew Cinder was a very special dog. He already owned another Rottweiler called Reeno and right away Cinder became the leader of the two dogs. She was devoted to Lorenzo and seemed to watch him wherever he went and whatever he did. He found her highly intelligent and very responsive to his training. Lorenzo and his wife, Roxanne, knew they had a good and faithful friend. But just how much of a friend Cinder turned out to be, no-one yet knew.

Early one May morning, when Cinder was around five years old, Lorenzo decided to go out on a four hour hike with his dogs. Both Cinder and Reeno barked excitedly as he put on his hiking boots and packed up his rucksack. Both animals loved their long walks with their master.

Lorenzo planned to take his pets along the rugged Mount Baldy trails that were close to his home. These treks were nothing new and on his days off, Lorenzo and his dogs would often go out hiking for a whole day.

Lorenzo said goodbye to Roxanne and set off. He was looking forward to a good long walk in the fresh air away from the stresses and strains of his job.

Half an hour later, though, Cinder began

behaving very strangely. She was usually way ahead of Lorenzo and Reeno, sniffing excitedly round for all the interesting smells and enjoying the freedom of the mountain trek. But today was different. For a reason her master couldn't understand, she lagged behind as if she was already tired, or worse still, sick. Lorenzo called her but she ignored him, once or twice even turning round and heading back home. At Lorenzo's command she would reluctantly turn back to follow him and continue their walk. But time and time again the dog turned for home. Eventually, afraid his beloved pet might be ill, Lorenzo decided to abandon his plans. He and Reeno turned back. This time Cinder was way ahead, anxious to get home.

Roxanne was surprised to see them back so soon. She had expected them to be gone at least until lunch time. She too was puzzled when her husband explained what had happened.

Lorenzo took Cinder into his living room and began to check her over. If there was something wrong with the Rottweiler he would have to call the vet. He looked in her ears, her eyes. He felt all over her limbs and ran his hand down her back. She seemed fine. She gazed up at him, loving all the attention she was getting, but looking a little puzzled. Lorenzo couldn't find a thing wrong with her. He patted her head and told her she was a silly girl. He expected her to go back out into her favourite place in the yard but she didn't. She continued to have that slightly puzzled look on her face as she stared at him. She stood as still as a statue as if she was waiting for something to happen. Lorenzo frowned. Something was bothering Cinder but he couldn't make out what it was. He was soon to find out.

Finally Lorenzo decided that he *would* call the vet after all. The dog was behaving very strangely and the sooner the vet tried to find out what was causing it, the better.

As Lorenzo stood up to go and use the cordless phone located on the kitchen worktop he suddenly began to feel very peculiar. There was an irregular pulse pounding like a drum in the side of his neck. He put his fingers up to feel it. His mind whirled. Lorenzo was trained in many aspects of emergency medicine and he knew at once that something was desperately wrong. His chest began to hurt. He felt as if someone had grabbed hold of his lungs and was trying to squeeze all the air out with tremendous force. He lurched forward, his hand outstretched for the phone but it was too late. Lorenzo collapsed to the floor and lost consciousness.

He had had a heart attack.

When Lorenzo came round, Reeno was licking his face. The dog knew something was desperately wrong with his master. He shouldn't be lying on the floor with his eyes closed. Cinder stood by, watching. It was then that she performed her miracle. As Reeno kept Lorenzo awake by licking his face, Cinder gave a great leap on to the worktop. She grabbed the phone and jumped down with it in her mouth. She took it to where Lorenzo lay, gasping and still in pain, hardly able to breathe. Barely conscious, he felt Cinder's nose pressing against his hand. Through his haze of pain and fear he realised the dog was trying to put the phone into his hand. Feeling it there, he managed to dial the American emergency number with his thumb. 911. He lay back, weak and exhausted from the effort. It had been as much as his strong body could do to dial the number.

The emergency operator answered straight away and Lorenzo just managed to gasp into the phone. 'I'm a fireman, I feel I'm having a heart attack.' All the time, Reeno was licking his face.

In one of the bedrooms down the hall, Roxanne was completely unaware of what was going on. She was shocked and amazed to hear the emergency ambulance screaming to a halt outside their house. She thought it must be a false alarm. But when she rushed out to tell Lorenzo about it she saw the reason why the vehicle had stopped there. Her hand flew to her mouth as she saw her husband lying on the floor with the two dogs beside him. She was just bending over him when the paramedics came through the door and began giving Lorenzo life-saving medication. When his condition had been stabilised they took him to hospital. He was there for four days. Helped by her pal, Reeno, Cinder had saved his life.

When he was feeling better, Lorenzo at last realised the reason for Cinder's strange behaviour that day on the mountain trail. She had realised that he was ill and knew that if a heart attack happened out there Lorenzo would certainly have died. Survival of an attack such as his depends upon rapid medication. Lorenzo said, 'I have no doubt that if I'd have kept on hiking, I wouldn't be here now.'

Cinder's heroism in saving her master's life was particularly miraculous because she had sensed something before it actually happened. Her closeness to Lorenzo had given her an uncanny ability to recognise some kind of change in his body chemistry. Some dogs, known as 'seizure dogs', are able to detect the onset of illness because the human body gives off a particular scent. This ability is the result of dog and human developing a really close bond such as the affection between Lorenzo and Cinder. That early May morning, Lorenzo's scent must have changed in some way and this alerted Cinder to the danger ahead. She was tuned in to his health and she knew he had a medical condition that Lorenzo himself wasn't aware of. When he finally came home from the hospital he put his medal of valour round Cinder's neck and gave her a great big hug and a kiss. He felt she deserved it.

But Cinder was to receive some medals of her own. Lorenzo had already been featured in the newspapers and magazines for his heroic acts of bravery in the course of his firefighting job and now it was Cinder's turn. She was nominated Dog Hero of the year by the Los Angeles Society for the Prevention of Cruelty to Animals, the highest award given by this organisation. She was named Dog of the Year by a magazine devoted to Rottweilers. She also received a special recognition award from the L.A. County Fire Department for her heroism.

Lorenzo was back at the fire department within a few weeks of his illness and carried on with his good work. He also spends a lot of time with his community, both on and off duty. He visits schools and youth clubs telling young people about the dangers of drugs and alcohol. His acts of bravery continue. A few months after his heart attack he rescued a dog from a burning building. Not only does he owe his life to man's best friend, one of man's best friends owes its life to him.

Lorenzo will never forget how Cinder, with Reeno, saved his life. Her intelligence and devotion brings awareness of how important man's best friend is to all of us. The Rottweiler's heroism represents all the amazing services that dogs are called upon to provide for the benefit of people.

At Lorenzo and Roxanne's home, Cinder's medals sit proudly alongside Lorenzo's and he and Cinder will always share that special love bond that enabled her to become a hero's hero.

BARRY
Heroic Search and Rescue Dog

A long time ago there was a monastery at the top of the great St Bernard pass through the mountains between Switzerland and Italy. The monks who lived in the monastery provided refuge for travellers between the two countries. In those days, there were no roads or tunnels to take you through the mountains and travellers had to use the natural pathways between the high peaks. In winter, these often got blocked by the bitter blizzards that swept the mountains and valleys. Many an unwary walker would become lost and disorientated and lots of them were never seen again.

The St Bernard monks used to give help as well as refuge to these Alpine travellers. They knew the mountains well and would often act as guides to people not sure of the way. And in the wintertime they would sometimes be called upon to search for lost travellers. This was very dangerous. Often the pathways were buried beneath several metres of snow, the freezing winds blew relentlessly through the mountain passes. But the monks were never afraid for they had help in their quests to find lost and injured people – their St Bernard dogs who lived in the monastery with them.

These dogs weren't like the huge St Bernards we see today. They were big and tough and had strong, broad chests although unlike today's dogs they had short legs, short, shaggy coats and broad feet that were good at walking through deep snow. Bred from Roman dogs that had lived in the area for centuries, they were loyal and brave, and devoted to their owners. They had a wonderful sense of smell and were very hardy. But one dog in particular, Barry, was the bravest and the hardiest of them all.

Barry was born in about 1800 and was one of a large litter of puppies who romped and played in the grounds of the monastery. To the monks, Barry seemed just the same as his brothers and sisters. He would growl and have pretend fights, yelp if he was hurt and run to his patient mother for comfort.

Nobody knew that Barry would one day become a very special dog indeed and that dozens of people would owe their lives to him.

Even at play, though, Barry was already showing his determined personality. He would hang on to a stick or bone long after the other puppies had let go. He had a very loud bark and never seemed to be afraid of anything.

When winter came, the monks saw how much Barry loved the snow. He was never scared of the wind moaning and whistling round the walls of the monastery or frightened of the blizzards that covered everything in a blanket of white. It was at this time that Barry's training began.

Although St Bernard dogs love snow and have a highly developed sense of smell, like any search dog they have to be trained to do what their masters command. First Barry had to learn to come when he was called. He had to obey the order to sit and stay, to lie down, to wait or to go forward. Barry learned all these things quickly and the monks were pleased with him. When they were confident he would do as he was told, he was taken out into the snow. Not to play this time but to learn how to walk without sinking into the deep drifts, to bark when commanded and to follow the scent of a monk who had been sent out before him. He had to learn to 'speak' when he found the man and to lead him back to the safety of the monastery. As well as all these things, like all St Bernards, Barry would clear away any snow from a person lying down and warm them with his own furry body until help arrived. In fact, Barry could do almost anything that was asked of him.

The monks were delighted. They could see that there was something very special about Barry. He was obedient and fast, he never let them down. What's more he was brave and courage was the most important quality a search and rescue dog needed.

Barry's bravery was to be tested sooner than anybody imagined.

When a group of travellers arrived at the monastery the monks sent Barry off with them on his first mission. It was a warm spring day although the mountains were still covered in deep snow and ice. The men needed guidance if they were to go safely through the pass. Barry was very excited. He seemed to know this was his first mission. After all his training, he had to prove himself. And although no-one realised it at the time, Barry was to do something that no-one could ever have trained him to do. He was to sense something and try to warn the travellers before it even happened.

Barry and the men were half way through the pass when disaster struck. Barry was trotting on ahead, pleased to be out in the mountains, pleased to be doing his job when he suddenly stopped dead. His head was tilted to one side, listening. The men could hear nothing and urged him forward. But then Barry began barking and racing around. He ran behind them and tried to herd them along faster. But they had heavy packs and couldn't hurry. They looked at one another muttering among themselves. Why had the monks trusted this novice dog to show them the way? They should have insisted on a more experienced one. Then, though,

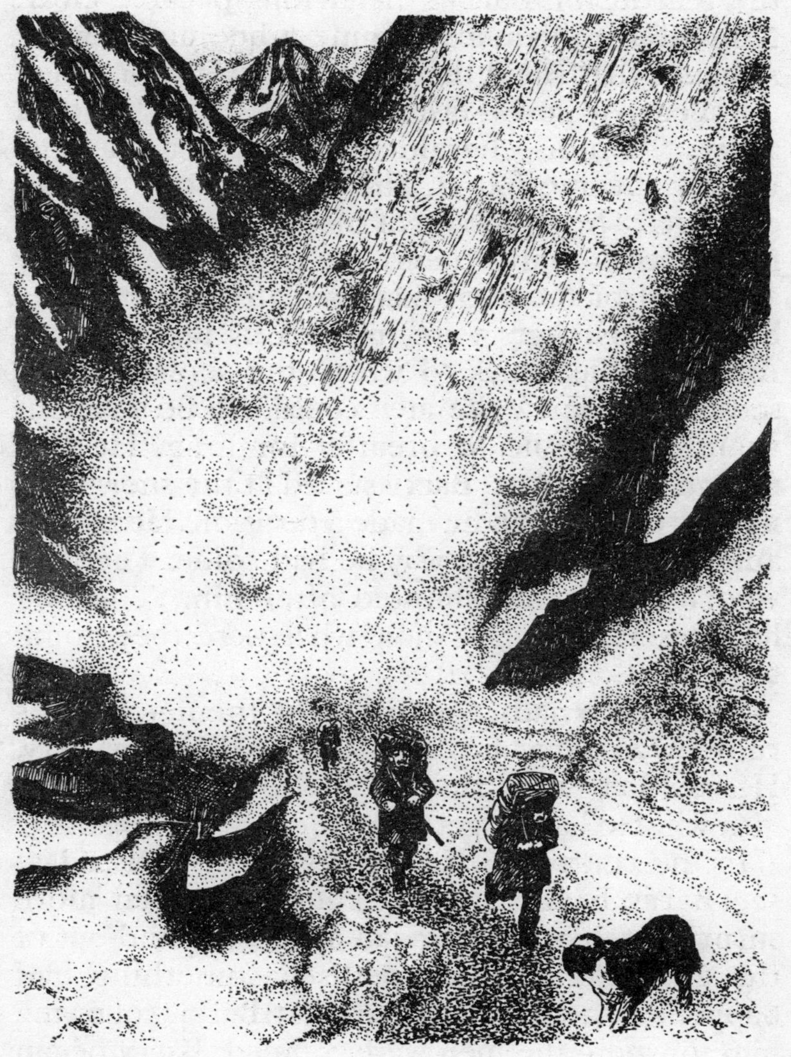

the reason for Barry's behaviour became clear. From above their heads came a booming sound. A sound that filled their hearts with terror. Then they began to run as fast as their heavy packs would allow. The noise heralded a massive avalanche. Up on the mountain, the warm sunshine had dislodged a huge amount of snow and it was hurtling downwards towards them.

Several of the men managed to dash to safety but several others were trapped by falling snow. Barry doubled back to where the snow was just settling. He knew the men could still be alive but wouldn't be able to breathe for long. He had to find them – fast. Barry stared at the snow for a minute or two then he made a decision. He turned and hurtled back the way he had come. The men who had escaped shouted after him. The dog had deserted them – now what were they going to do?

But Barry hadn't abandoned them – he was running as fast as he could back to the monastery. He couldn't tackle finding all the buried men on his own. He had to get help.

In the courtyard, the monks were surprised to see Barry back so soon. They were even more surprised when the dog ran around, in and out of the gate. Finally they realised something had happened and they hurried after Barry, following him to where the men were trapped. Barry began digging frantically. The monks and the other travellers helped. Soon, all the trapped men were free. Barry was a hero.

Back at the monastery, the monks knew they had been right about Barry. He was a very special dog indeed. That night they made a big fuss of him. He had a special dinner and was allowed to lie by the fire in the great hall. The monks knew they had a treasure.

There are many stories of Barry's heroism during his twelve years as a search and rescue mountain dog. He once saved a little girl who had become lost in the snow. He didn't run back to alert the monks but seemed to know she would freeze to death if he left her alone. He lay down beside her and kept her warm, then when she was feeling better he allowed her to climb on to his back and ride home to safety. Another time he searched for and found a little boy who had fallen down a crevasse. The boy was trapped on a ledge of ice. Barry was able to reach down and drag him to safety before he slid off and plunged to his death.

Barry soon became famous for his devotion to duty. People on both sides of the mountains heard the stories of his bravery. Barry didn't know he had become a star and continued helping travellers until the cold weather and hard work began to take its toll on his health. The St Bernard had been working for many years and he began to grow slow and stiff. In all he had helped to save the lives of over forty people.

Finally the monks decided that Barry should retire. They asked one of their friends who lived in Berne if he would take Barry to live with him. They wanted their dear old dog to spend the last years of his life in warmth and comfort. Barry stayed in Berne for the rest of his life. As he lay by the fire the monks' friend often wondered if Barry ever thought about his days spent searching and rescuing ill-fated travellers or if he knew what a great hero he had become.

The St Bernard monks have never forgotten Barry and to this day the best of every litter of puppies born at the monastery is named Barry in honour of the great dog. They believe this serves as a symbol of the unselfish work performed by so many dogs in the service of man.

Today, quite a different kind of rescue dog is used. After the Second World War, the Swiss army trained four German Shepherd dogs to search for victims of avalanches, so following in Barry's paw-steps. This was so successful that many dog training centres were set up in the Alps. Then a Scotsman brought the idea back to Britain. Not only were German Shepherds used but also Border Collies and Labradors.

Now, search and rescue dogs are used all over the world and in all kinds of situations. From the high fells of Britain to the snowy mountains of Europe and America, dogs of all breeds are used to search out and rescue lost or injured people. Dogs are used after earthquakes and bombings to seek out victims, alive or dead. No-one really knows how a dog can smell a person who may be buried under tons of snow or rubble but this uncanny ability has saved many hundreds of lives.

The monks and the big St Bernard dogs still live high up in the Alps although they are no longer needed to guide travellers to safety.

Outside the Museum of Natural History in Berne stands a statue of Barry. He doesn't carry a small cask of brandy as popularly believed. In fact St Bernard's never did carry them. But what the statue of Barry does carry is a sense of courage and determination and devotion to duty that is typical of every search and rescue dog that is used to help man in the world today.

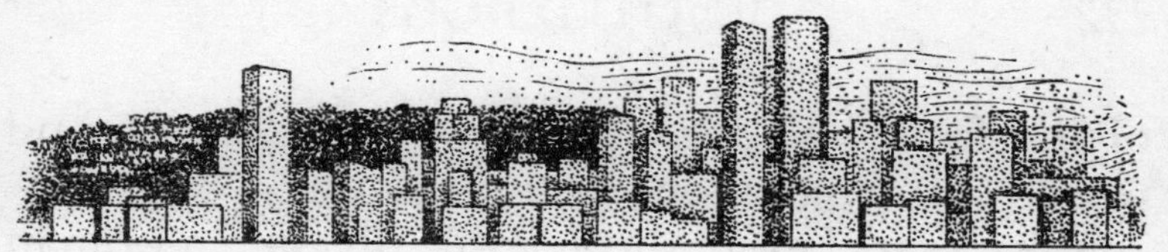

CINNAMON
Earthquake Dog

The citizens of Mexico City will never forget the month of September, 1985, for it was then that a major earthquake devastated their city. Thousands of lives were lost and the streets and avenues were in ruins. Many heroic stories arose from that tragedy and many of these were about the brave search and rescue dog teams that worked tirelessly to seek out trapped victims, in many cases saving their lives.

Thirteen teams of dogs and their handlers were drafted in from all over the United States. They soon learned what a difficult task lay ahead. In the industrial area of the city, many people were trapped beneath several floors of steel and concrete and hopes for their survival were slim. As the days went by, any chance that anyone would be found alive were fading fast. However, what a group of desperate people trapped beneath the ruins of one of the factories didn't know was that search and rescue dog Cinnamon was on her way.

A few years before this terrible disaster, a woman called Shirley Hammond decided to move house. She and her family wanted to live near the coast and decided to make their home on the outskirts of San Francisco, California. Shirley was a dog lover and had owned search and rescue dogs for many years.

The move to California proved to be a good one. The area was beautiful, just what Shirley and her husband had often dreamed of. There was only one snag – there were reports of motorbike gangs threatening residents of the area where Shirley and her family had bought their house. A neighbour owned a Doberman for protection. Shirley fell in love with the animal and decided to buy one herself. She could think of no better dog to protect her family than this fiercely loyal breed. This dog was Nina and she became Shirley's first Doberman search and rescue dog.

Then Shirley bought Cinnamon, the dog who was to work so tirelessly and bravely in the aftermath of the Mexico City earthquake.

When Cinnamon was fully trained, she and Shirley went on many missions together but this turned out to be one of the most scary. When they arrived in what was left of the city, Shirley felt a shudder of apprehension. She and Cinnamon and other teams from the Search and Rescue Association had been assigned to a devastated factory where it was believed people were trapped and might possibly still be alive. Only a short while before, the building had been several stories high. Now it was a jungle of fallen concrete and steel. Worse still, the city was still getting after-shocks and as Shirley and Cinnamon crawled carefully into the ruins, the earth began to vibrate once more.

When this happened Shirley's stomach turned with fear. Cinnamon whined softly. She knew she had a job to do but couldn't understand why the earth was shaking. She was scared of the noise and the air full of dust and dirt. It's well known that dogs can sense earthquakes before they even happen. To be in the middle of one was terrifying.

Shirley took a deep breath. Would Cinnamon be brave enough to overcome her fear and do the job she was trained to do? She reminded herself of all the missions she and the Doberman had done together. They had been in many dangerous situations. She gave Cinnamon a reassuring hug. They'd got a vital job to do and they'd better get on with it. Many lives could be at stake. If there really were people beneath that rubble then Cinnamon could be their only chance of survival.

As Shirley and her dog made their way cautiously down into the depths of the building the aftershocks began again. Bits of masonry began falling all around them. There had only been a soft rumble at first but now it began in earnest. Cinnamon whined again as the building shook and shuddered. It was all Shirley could do to keep her cool. She murmured words of comfort to Cinnamon. The success of missions like this depend upon the close bond between handler and dog. Cinnamon would only work well if Shirley showed confidence and calmness. The dog would sense any emotion her handler was feeling. Sadness, joy, uncertainty, fear. Shirley knew her dog would read her terror and feel scared too. She *must* stay focused and so must her dog.

As they moved forward Shirley took a deep breath. Her regular job as a critical care nurse had prepared her for traumatic situations. She knew *this* one was going to test her skills to the limit.

Shirley and Cinnamon had been in tumbledown buildings before. Part of the dog's training had been to pick up scents from all kinds of surfaces. But this was different. Great blocks of concrete lay scattered all over the place, broken glass, smashed machinery, electrical wires sticking out everywhere. As the aftershocks went on and on Shirley began to wonder if they would ever stop. The factory was located in the central district of the city where the earthquake was at its worst. It was built on a drained lake bed that transmitted tremors more easily than other types of terrain.

Shirley took a few more seconds to pull herself together then tried to work out how she and

Cinnamon were to navigate the ruins.

Before they had gone in, one of the other disaster teams had reported hearing shouts from between the floors that had collapsed and it was here that Shirley and Cinnamon headed. Shirley had to crawl on her hands and knees. The gap was barely more than a metre and with each wave of aftershock it got smaller. Shirley began to wonder not only if they were going to be able to get in but if they were ever going to get out again.

Shirley watched as Cinnamon crawled ahead of her across a sea of broken masonry. She had overcome her fear of the shuddering building. Her ears were up and her tail wagging frantically.

Shirley's heart beat faster with excitement. Then the Doberman began sniffing and pawing at an area of rubble. This was her alert sign. She was telling Shirley she had found human scent. *Live* human scent. Shirley's hand shook as she breathlessly called the team on her mobile radio. She had to tell them what had happened and call for another dog to confirm Cinnamon's alert before they could summon teams of diggers to try to get the victims out. After she had made the call, she hugged Cinnamon and made a great big fuss of her before they both crawled thankfully out of the building.

Soon, another team arrived. Peter with his dog, Alex. Shirley quickly explained the situation and they disappeared inside. Shirley thought it was the longest ten minutes of her life as she and Cinnamon waited anxiously for Peter to call her up on the radio. Then she heard what she hoped to hear. Cinnamon had been right, there *were* people alive down there. Alex had alerted at the same place. Shirley hugged and kissed Cinnamon, her confidence in her dog had been rewarded. She knew Cinnamon had been scared and was doubly proud of the dog who had overcome her own terror to save the lives of others.

Shirley was even more proud of Cinnamon when twelve days later she learned that the earthquake victims her dog had found were finally rescued. Eight people of the twelve who had been buried, had survived. Cinnamon was a hero!

Shirley and her dogs are members of the Type 2 Canine Search Specialist team. She and one of her other dogs, Spice, were called to search for victims of a bomb that exploded in Oklahoma city some years later. Shirley is full of admiration and love for her animals. She is proud to be the handler of such clever and gallant dogs. She knows that if it wasn't for them, and for the other search and rescue dogs who are called upon to work in disasters and accidents all over the world, many hundreds of people would not be alive today.

DEVOTED DOGS
further reading

You can find out more about the dogs in these stories, and other devoted dogs too, in these books which might be in your local library or bookshop:

Rats, the Story of a Dog Soldier by Max Holdstock
(Chivers Press)

Moobli by Mike Tomkies
(Jonathan Cape Ltd.)

Greyfriars Bobby – the Real Story at Last by Forbes Macgregor
(Gordon Wright Publishing)

Clever and Courageous Dogs by Winifred Finlay and Gillian Hancock
(Kay & Ward)

Heroic Dogs by Lesley Scott Ordish
(Arlington Books)

Bothie, the Polar Dog by Ranulph Fiennes
(Mandarin)

TRUE ANIMAL STORIES
Heroic Horses

Sue Welford

Meet Goldflake *who travelled from Lands End to John O'Groats* . . . Sefton, *the brave army horse – even a terrorist bomb couldn't stop him* . . . Witez II, *the Arabian stallion who survived the Second World War and founded a dynasty* . . .

Including the classic story of Alexander the Great's black stallion Bucephalus, and Red Rum, the record breaker, here are ten exhilarating stories of horses who proved their heroism beyond a doubt!

ORDER FORM

Sue Welford

0 340 74420 0   TRUE ANIMAL STORIES: *HEROIC HORSES*   £3.99 ☐

Lucy Daniels

0 340 70438 1   JESS THE BORDER COLLIE 1: *THE ARRIVAL*   £3.99 ☐
0 340 70439 x   JESS THE BORDER COLLIE 2: *THE CHALLENGE*   £3.99 ☐
0 340 70440 3   JESS THE BORDER COLLIE 3: *THE RUNAWAY*   £3.99 ☐

All Hodder Children's books are available at your local bookshop, or can be ordered direct from the publisher. Just tick the titles you would like and complete the details below. Prices and availability are subject to change without prior notice.

Please enclose a cheque or postal order made payable to *Bookpoint Ltd*, and send to: Hodder Children's Books, 39 Milton Park, Abingdon, OXON OX14 4TD, UK.
Email Address: orders@bookpoint.co.uk

If you would prefer to pay by credit card, our call centre team would be delighted to take your order by telephone. Our direct line *01235 400414* (lines open 9.00 am–6.00 pm Monday to Saturday, 24 hour message answering service). Alternatively you can send a fax on *01235 400454*.

TITLE		FIRST NAME		SURNAME	

ADDRESS	
DAYTIME TEL:		POST CODE	

If you would prefer to pay by credit card, please complete:
Please debit my Visa/Access/Diner's Card/American Express (delete as applicable) card no:

Signature .... Expiry Date: ....

If you would NOT like to receive further information on our products please tick the box.   ☐